PENGUIN

BLIND OWL

SADEQ HEDAYAT was born in Tehran in 1903 and is considered one of the most important Iranian prose writers of the twentieth century. He is celebrated as the father of modernist Persian literature and is credited with bringing modern Persian literature onto the international scene. Although born into a prominent aristocratic family, Hedayat's writings display an obsession with characters who populate the fringes of society—the base and the marginalized. In 1936, while living in Bombay, he published his most famous work, *Blind Owl*, as a handwritten volume with original illustrations. Hedayat took his own life in Paris in 1951. Despite his short literary life, Hedayat was a prolific writer and leaves behind a copious body of work.

SASSAN TABATABAI was born in Tehran in 1967 and has been living in the United States since 1980. He is a poet, a translator, and a scholar of medieval Persian literature. He is Master Lecturer in World Languages and Literatures and the Core Curriculum, and Coordinator of the Persian Language Program, at Boston University. Tabatabai is the author of *Father of Persian Verse: Rudaki and His Poetry* (Leiden University Press, 2010), *Uzunburun: Poems* (Pen and Anvil Press, 2011), and *Sufi Haiku* (Nemi Books, 2021).

SADEQ HEDAYAT

Blind Owl

Translated with an Introduction by
SASSAN TABATABAI

PENGUIN BOOKS

PENGUIN BOOKS

An imprint of Penguin Random House LLC
penguinrandomhouse.com

Originally self-published in Persian as *Boo-e-koor* in Mumbai, formerly Bombay, 1936.

LIBRARY OF CONGRESS CATALOGING-IN-PUBLICATION DATA
Names: Hidāyat, Ṣādiq, 1903-1951, author. | Tabatabai, Sassan, 1967–
translator author of introduction.
Title: Blind owl / Sadeq Hedayat ; translated with an introduction by Sassan Tabatabai.
Other titles: Būf-i kūr. English
Description: New York : Penguin Classics, 2022. |
Includes bibliographical references.
Identifiers: LCCN 2021031212 (print) | LCCN 2021031213 (ebook) |
ISBN 9780143136583 (paperback) | ISBN 9780525508083 (ebook)
Subjects: LCGFT: Novels.
Classification: LCC PK6561.H4 B813 2022 (print) |
LCC PK6561.H4 (ebook) | DDC 891/.5533—dc23
LC record available at https://lccn.loc.gov/2021031212
LC ebook record available at https://lccn.loc.gov/2021031213

Printed in the United States of America

Set in Sabon LT Pro

Contents

BLIND OWL

Contents

Introduction

On April 9, 1951, Parisian police were called to a small flat on 37 Rue de Championnet. There they found the dead body of a forty-eight-year-old Iranian writer identified as Sadeq Hedayat, who had apparently committed suicide by gas inhalation. He was found lying on a blanket on the floor of the small kitchen in his apartment. He had sealed the flat to keep the gas from escaping the room as best he could. There was no suicide note. Thus ended the life of one of the most consequential Iranian prose writers of the twentieth century.

Sadeq Hedayat is generally lauded as the father of modernist Persian literature. He is seen as the inheritor of the mantle of Mohammad-Ali Jamalzadeh, the great Persian prose writer of the turn of the century, and is credited with bringing modern Persian literature onto the international scene. Although born into a prominent aristocratic family, his writings display an obsession with characters who populate the fringes of society—the base and the marginalized. Hedayat came of age in the period following Iran's Constitutional Revolution of 1906, but his most prolific years as a writer coincided with the reign of Reza Shah, who ruled Iran as the founder of the Pahlavi dynasty from 1925 until his forced abdication by the Allies in 1941. This was a period of

autocracy in Iran when freedom of speech was severely re-
stricted. In this environment, some intellectuals embraced
the new regime and were rewarded accordingly with government positions and comfortable lives, whereas others took
an active stance against the curtailed freedoms and the re-
strictive atmosphere and revolted against the establishment.
Hedayat, as a man with little respect for sycophancy and the
privileges enjoyed by the upper class, shunned the former
group, and as a recluse who kept society at arm's length, did
not join the latter. Instead, he took refuge in the solitary enterprise of the writer. His writings reflect a disdain for both
the monarchy and the clerical establishment in Iran. The
theme of a people abused by these two powers is a prevalent
feature of his works.

Sadeq Hedayat was born on February 17, 1903, in Tehran,
Iran, and was educated in Tehran's College Saint-Louis (a
French Catholic school). In 1925, he received a scholarship
to be part of a group of Iranian students to continue their
higher education in France. After a number of false starts in
different fields, in 1927, a disillusioned Hedayat attempted
suicide by throwing himself into the river Marne. In 1930,
he returned to Iran without having acquired a degree. Around
this time, he started writing *Blind Owl*, which would become his most famous work. In 1936, Hedayat moved to
Bombay to live with the Parsi community and study Zoroastrianism and Pahlavi (Middle Persian). In the same year, he
published *Blind Owl* as a handwritten volume with original
illustrations. Only fifty mimeographed copies were made of
this edition. He returned to Paris in 1950, where he took his
own life on April 9 of the following year.

During his short literary life, Hedayat dedicated himself

to the study of Western literature, in particular the works
of Kafka, Sartre, Chekhov, and Gogol, and showed great interest in Iranian folklore, Zoroastrianism, and the Pahlavi
language (he published a work titled, "Pahlavi Script and
Phonetic Alphabet"). Hedayat eventually became one of the
central figures in Iranian intellectual circles and joined the
literary group known as *Rab'eh* ("Group of Four"), which
also included Mas'ud Farzad, Mojtaba Minovi and Bozorg
Alavi. Despite his short literary life, Hedayat was a prolific
writer and published a wide range of material, including
short stories, plays, travelogues, satires, literary criticism,
studies in Persian folklore, and translations from both French
and Pahlavi. He is buried in Père Lachaise cemetery in Paris.
Hedayat is justifiably considered one of the greatest Iranian
writers of the twentieth century.

**Note: The following pages contain details of the story that
can spoil the plot. The first-time reader of *Blind Owl* is
urged to skip over this part of the Introduction and return to
it after having read the novel.**

Blind Owl tells the story of an isolated narrator with a fragile relationship with time and reality, who relates his own
story in the first person, in a string of hazy, dreamlike recollections. The book is divided into two main parts, each of
which is followed by a transitional passage that shifts the
time and space of the narrative.

    In the first part, we are introduced to the unnamed pro-
tagonist, a painter of pen-case covers who lives alone in a
remote and uninhabited area on the outskirts of an unnamed
city. In the opening pages, he tells us that he is trying to re-
late the story of one incident from his life that has left an

enduring, "poisoned" mark on him. He is writing what he remembers, not for the sake of posterity but in order to get to know himself better. The reason he is writing his recollections, he tells us, "is to introduce myself to my shadow—which is hunched over on the wall and swallows everything I write with a voracious appetite."

The narrator always paints the exact same scene on the pen cases: a hunched old man wearing a cape and turban sitting under a cypress tree, separated by a small stream from a beautiful young woman in black who is bending down to offer him a water lily. One day, a man comes to his door and identifies himself as the uncle who he has never seen. He is a hunched old man wearing a cape and turban. Our protagonist realizes the only thing he has in his house to offer his uncle is a flask of aged wine that was his birthright. When he goes to fetch it, he sees the same scene he has been painting on the pen cases through an opening in the pantry.

He is struck by the young woman's "intoxicating" eyes, that seemed to have "witnessed horrifying, supernatural scenes others can't see," and terrified by the old man's "dry, disturbing laugh that made the hair of your body stand on end." The scene (along with the opening in the pantry) subsequently disappears, which sends him down the path of delirium. Every night he prowls around his house trying to find the cypress tree by the stream, but to no avail.

One night the narrator returns to find the same woman outside the door of his house. She enters and lies down on his bed. He wants to offer her something but realizes he only has the flask of aged wine. He pours a cup of wine through her clenched teeth as she appears to be sleeping. Soon he realizes that she is not sleeping but is dead. He repeatedly tries to sketch her face on paper but is unable to do so because he cannot see her eyes. Suddenly, she seems to come back to life and momentarily opens her eyes long enough for him to sketch them on paper. Now it is clear that she is dead and apparently has been dead for some time because her body is starting to decompose and there are maggots crawling on her.

Unsure of what to do with a decomposing corpse, the narrator decides to chop up her body and put her in a suitcase and bury her. At this moment a mysterious gravedigger appears with a hearse-wagon and offers his help. The gravedigger is a hunched old man wearing a cape and turban and has a dry and disturbing laugh that makes the hair of your body stand on end. In the process of digging the grave, the old man unearths a glazed earthen jug, which he identifies as a vase from Rhages, and gives it to the narrator. This is the first indication of the setting for the story. Rhages is the classical name for the city of Rey, which dates back to the time of the Medes in the seventh and eighth centuries BCE. Once back in his house, our narrator unwraps the vase from a filthy piece of cloth and sees the image of a woman painted on it. He is shocked to discover that the image of the woman on the vase is identical to his own sketch on paper. The first part of the story ends with the narrator sitting in front of his opium brazier. He smokes all his remaining opium and seems to drift off in a fevered, semiconscious dream.

The first part of the story is followed by a brief transitional link in which the narrator claims to have been reborn into a different world, "an ancient world but one closer and more natural." His clothes are torn and he is covered in blood, and feeling paranoid that the police will burst in at any moment to arrest him. But instead of trying to get rid of the bloodstains, he is overwhelmed by the urge to write down his recollections in order to "expel the demon" that has been torturing him.

The second part of the story opens with quotation marks that don't close until the very end of the section, reminding the reader that this is a testament written down by the narrator himself. It is not clear whether this part of the story constitutes an actual movement back in time and offers a window into a previous incarnation, or if it signifies confessional recollections of a hallucinatory world fueled by opium. Nevertheless, the narrative that unfolds provides the disturbing perspective, supported by clues, that eventually unlocks the mysteries to the enigmatic accounts of the first part.

We realize that the narrator does not live alone on the outskirts of the city, but lives with his old wet nurse and unfaithful wife (who is also his first cousin) in the city of Rey. He suffers from an ailment that, for the most part, has him confined to his coffin-like room where he languishes like a living corpse. From the window in his room that faces the street, he can see a butcher shop and an old peddler who sells all kinds of oddments. In the solitude of his room, the narrator becomes increasingly obsessed with the butcher and the peddler, who infiltrate his psyche like termites and slowly eat away at him from the inside.

The narrator lives an isolated life from his wife, who has refused to consummate their marriage and who does not even let him kiss her. Always lurking in the backdrop of his thoughts is his own sense of inadequacy and the paranoia that a group of drunken patrolmen will burst in at any moment and arrest him. Soon he discovers, what he thinks, is the cause of his wife's refusal of him. She has numerous lovers, who he calls her "fornicators," and is showing signs of pregnancy. He develops a love-hate relationship with her and is tormented by the thought of losing her.

Eventually, he is horrified to find out that one of his wife's fornicators is the old peddler. But as has been the case throughout the story, it's not exactly clear what is real and what is a product of his paranoia. Finally, he disguises himself as the peddler by wrapping a dirty scarf around his face and visits his wife in her room with a bone-handled knife that he is hiding under his cloak. There is a violent sex scene during which the narrator "inadvertently" stabs and kills her. The story ends with the narrator looking into the mirror only to be confronted by the old peddler of oddments with the disturbing laugh.

In the final transitional passage after the second part, the narrator once again finds himself in the same familiar room he had occupied in the first part. The opium brazier in front of him is cold and full of spent charcoal. He sees his own reflection in the mirror covered in coagulated blood with maggots wriggling on him.

Throughout the work, emanations of the two archetypal characters on the pen-case covers from the first part of the story—the hunched old man with the disturbing laugh, and the beautiful woman in black with the intoxicating eyes—reappear through repetitive turns of phrase that draw the reader into the unstable psyche of a tortured soul whose life unfolds in the dark recesses of his mind. The gravedigger, the butcher, the peddler of oddments, the narrator's uncle, his father-in-law, and ultimately the narrator himself are different manifestations of the hunched old man. The mysterious ethereal woman who comes to his house in the first part of the story, and the narrator's mother—a temple dancer in

India named Bugam Dasi (the only named character in the book)—are idealized images of the young woman in black, whereas the narrator's wife, who he calls "the slut," is a demonized reflection of the same character.

The misogyny with which the narrator engages his wife in the second part of the story stands in stark contrast to his attitude toward the ethereal woman of the first part and his mother, from the second part. The narrator is consumed by the ethereal woman who embodies a vision of purity that must "not be sullied by the eyes of a stranger" or touched by earthly hands lest she wither and die. The only physical contact he has with her is in his bed with her dead body, initially, in a scene that suggests necrophilia and subsequently, when he dismembers her dead body in order to put her in his suitcase. Finally, he ends up burying her in a remote location and covers up the grave so well that even he himself cannot tell where she is buried. His wife, on the other hand, who has a number of sexual partners, is the epitome of a sullied woman as she is seen and touched by multiple strangers, something that fuels his sense of solitude and inadequacy.

When the narrator recounts the story of his mother, Bugam Dasi, in the second part, she is a virgin in the service of the temple of Lingam Puja. Eventually, she is corrupted by the narrator's father/uncle and is dismissed from the temple when she becomes pregnant with the narrator. In contrast, the narrator's wife is depicted as the corrupting agent who is not a virgin when they get married and eventually becomes pregnant by someone other the narrator. She is presented as calculating and opportunistic and the root of all his woes. In turn, he directs all his lust and rage at her. He suspects that she manipulated him in order to force him to marry her, so that she could take possession of the house where they live together after his death, something that seems increasingly impending as the story unfolds and his health deteriorates. Her plan is ultimately foiled when she has a miscarriage.

Other than the different emanations of the two main characters, several items create a bridge between the two parts of the story. The glazed vase from Rhages, which the gravedigger unearths and subsequently gives to the narrator in the first part, reappears in the second part in the spread in front of the old peddler of oddments and is one of the indicators of a possible shift in time frames between the two sections. In the first part, the narrator offers the gravedigger two qiran and one abasi, Iranian coins that were in circulation until the early 1930s. In the second part, we are told that the peddler was a potter in his youth and had only kept that one vase for himself. The narrator buys the vase from him for two dirhem and four pashiz coins, which were in circulation during the Sassanian Empire in the third century CE.

In the second part of the story, we learn the history behind the flask of aged wine from the first part. The wine, which is the narrator's birthright, contains the same snake venom that was responsible for the death of the narrator's father or uncle. In the first part, the narrator dismembers the dead body of the young woman with a bone-handled knife. In the second part, he murders his wife with a bone-handled knife.

The details the reader encounters in the second part of the story provide clues that help unlock some of the mysteries in the first part: the appearance of the uncle, the narrator's relationship with the woman who randomly shows up at his door, her death, and ultimately, the disturbing reality about her momentarily opening her eyes after she is already dead. The fascinating architecture of the book lends the story to more than one reading. For a full appreciation of the interwoven narrative between the two parts, the reader is encouraged to revisit the first part of the story after reading the entire book.

As the second part of the story progresses, the more the narrator sinks into paranoia and delusion, the more he identifies with the butcher and the peddler. Before the final sequence of the story, in which he finally acts on his conflicted feelings of love and hatred toward his wife, he sees his own bent shadow on the wall that looks like an owl, a blind owl. In the Iranian tradition, the owl is seen as an inauspicious bird, an omen of bad fortune that is associated with ruin and decay. The appearance of the blind owl as a reflection of the narrator initiates the final tragedy of the story.

Since its inception, *Blind Owl* has had a tumultuous reception in Iran. In 1936, while living in Bombay, Hedayat printed fifty mimeographed copies of his handwritten manuscript of *Blind Owl* (the so-called Bombay Edition) for private distribution. Confident that the publication of the book would be banned by the government in Iran, he printed "Not for sale or distribution in Iran" on the inside cover. The first publication of *Blind Owl* in Iran was a censored edition that appeared in serial form in the journal *Iran* from 1941 to 1942. Over the years, a number of censored editions were published, until 2005, when publication of the book was completely banned in the country. To this date, *Blind Owl* has been translated into Armenian, Dutch, English, French, Filipino, Finnish, German, Indonesian, Japanese, Malayalam, Polish, Romanian, Spanish, Turkish, and Urdu.

Over the years, especially after Hedayat's suicide, a myth developed in Iran around *Blind Owl*, with people repeating a largely baseless sentiment that reading this book is a dangerous enterprise and can lead the reader to commit suicide. A large part of this was probably perpetuated by an uninformed public who associated the author with his created work. It is clear that Hedayat battled his own demons that eventually led to his suicide. But to consider his suicide as somehow prompting others to follow suit is an unfounded assertion. Undoubtedly, some of the misconception about the "danger" of reading the book is also steeped in the nihilistic outlook of the narrator himself, who sees death as a panacea for the angst-ridden misery of his life. He repeatedly yearns for the oblivion that death would provide, and on several occasions, contemplates downing a cup of the poisoned wine to end it all. Nevertheless, he is a character who, in the end, is capable of homicide but not suicide.

As a basis for my translation of *Blind Owl*, I have used a copy of Hedayat's original handwritten manuscript of the 1936 Bombay Edition. The Sadeq Hedayat Foundation in Iran considers this edition to be the most reliable, and only unaltered text of *Blind Owl*.

In my translation, I have tried to carry over Hedayat's conversational voice and colloquial use of language by maintaining, as much as possible, his at times seemingly endless sentences, his heavy use of em dashes, as well as the haunting repetitions and formulaic turns of phrase that echo throughout the work.

SASSAN TABATABAI

Suggestions for Further Reading

Azadibougar, Omid. "The Serious Century and Hedayat's Grim
    Laughter." *Iranian Studies* 47, no. 1 (2014).

Bashiri, Iraj. 1974. *Hedayat's Ivory Tower: Structural Analysis of*
    The Blind Owl. Minneapolis, MN: Manor House.

Beard, Michael. 1990. *Hedayat's "Blind Owl" as a Western*
    Novel. Princeton, NJ: Princeton University Press.

_____. "Hedāyat's *The Blind Owl* Forty Years After." *World*
    Literature Today 53, no. 4 (1979).

Cisco, Michael. "Eternal Recurrence in *The Blind Owl*." *Iranian*
    Studies 43, no. 4 (2010).

Coulter, Yasamine C. "A Comparative Post-Colonial Approach to
    Hedayat's The Blind Owl." *Comparative Literature and Cul-*
    ture 2, no. 3 (2000).

Elahi, Babak. "Poisons and Remedies in Sadegh Hedayat's *The*
    Blind Owl." *Middle Eastern Literatures* 15, no. 2 (2012).

Ghanoonparvar, M. R. "Sadeq Hedayat, His Work and His Won-
    drous World." *Iranian Studies* 43, no. 4 (2010).

Hillmann, Michael, ed. 1978. *Hedayat's* The Blind Owl *Forty*
    Years Later. Austin: University of Texas Press.

Kamshad, Hassan. 1966. *Modern Persian Prose Literature.* Cam-
    bridge: Cambridge University Press.

Katouzian, Homa. 1991. *Sadeq Hedayat: The Life and Legend of an Iranian Writer*. New York: I.B. Tauris.

_____. "Precedents of *The Blind Owl*." *Middle Eastern Literatures* 15, no. 2 (2012).

Mansouri-Zeyni, Sina. "Haunting Language-Game: Baudrillardian Metamorphoses in Sadeq Hedayat's *The Blind Owl*." *Iranian Studies* 46, no. 4 (2013).

Turan, Oktay. "Spaces of Suicide: Architectural Metaphors and Leitmotifs in Sadeq Hedayat's *Blind Owl*." *Journal of Architecture* (London, England) 12, no. 2 (2007).

Wanberg, Kyle. 2020. "Disorientation and Horror in Sadeq Hedayat's *The Blind Owl*." In *Maps of Empire: A Topography of World Literature*, 94. Toronto: University of Toronto Press.

"Hedayat, Sadeq." 2003 (last updated 2013). *Encyclopaedia Iranica*. Vol. XII, Fasc. 1 New York.

Blind Owl

Blind Owl

In life there are wounds that like termites, slowly bore into and eat away at the isolated soul. You can't tell anyone about these pains. People think of them as strange and unnatural, and if you try to talk or write about them, they fall back on their same worn beliefs and dismiss them with a mocking smile. That's because man has not yet found any solution, any drug that can cure them. The only cure can be found in the amnesia brought on by wine and the artificial sleep of opium. But alas, these remedies are short-lived, and instead of relief, after a short time they only add to the pain. One day, will someone be able to discover the secret to these supernatural events, when the shadow of the soul languishes in the purgatory between sleep and wakefulness?

I will only describe one of these events that happened to me and shook me so violently I will never forget it. It has poisoned my life and I will carry its cursed mark on me to the end of my days. Did I say poisoned? I meant to say it is a grief from which I have always suffered and always will.

I will try to write down everything I remember from the chain of events. Maybe I will be able to make sense of them and actually believe them myself. It makes no difference to me if others believe me or not. The only thing that scares me is that I will die tomorrow without having known myself. In life, I have encountered a dark abyss that separates me from others. I understand that as much as possible, I must remain extinguished and keep my thoughts to myself. And if I have decided to write them down now, it is only to introduce myself to my shadow—which is hunched over on the wall and swallows everything I write with a voracious appetite—it is for him that I want to conduct an experiment: maybe we can get to know each other better. Since I've cut off my ties with everyone else, I want to get to know myself better.

Hollow thoughts! Maybe. But they torture me more than any reality. People out there like me, who apparently have the same needs and desires, are they not here to fool me? Are they not shadows created just to fool and mock me? Is everything I feel, see, judge, not just fiction that has nothing to do with reality?

I only write for my own shadow who sits on the wall against the light. I have to introduce myself to him.

In this cruel world, full of poverty and misery, I thought that for the first time a beam of sunlight had broken through to my life. But alas, it wasn't a beam of light. It was only a fleeting ray, a shooting star that appeared to me in the form of a woman—or an angel—and in the brightness of that one moment, that one second, I witnessed all the miseries of my life and discovered their grandeur. Then this fleeting apparition disappeared into the black whirlpool into which she was destined to disappear. No, I was not able to keep this fleeting apparition for myself.

Three months! No, it had been two months and four days since I lost her trail, but the memory of her bewitching eyes—the lethal spark in her eyes—has always stayed with me. How can I forget her? How can I forget someone so attached to my life?

No, I will never utter her name. Because her slim, ethereal figure, her large questioning eyes in whose bright gaze my painful life was slowly melting away, no longer belongs to this base, vicious world. No, her name must not be sullied with the things of this earth.

After her, I completely withdrew from the company of others. I completely withdrew from the company of the stupid and the fortunate, and sought shelter in the amnesia of wine and opium. My entire life has passed and passes within the four walls of my room. My entire life has passed within these four walls.

I spent my days painting pen-case covers—I spent all my time only painting pen-case covers and consuming wine and opium. I had chosen the pathetic occupation of painting pen-case covers to distract myself, to kill time.

It so happens that my house is situated outside the city in a calm and quiet place far from the hustle and bustle of people's lives. It is completely isolated with no other development in sight. Only from that side you can see a row of flat, down-pressed clay homes, and then the city starts. I don't know what idiot with poor taste, in what prehistoric times built this house. When I close my eyes, not only do I still see all its nooks and crannies, but I feel their weight on my shoulders. It is the kind of house that could only have been painted on old pen-case covers.

I must write all this down to make sure I hadn't imagined everything. I have to explain everything to my shadow on the wall. Yes—it was the only thing that kept me going. Surrounded by the four walls of my room, I painted pen cases and wasted my time in that pathetic hobby. But after I saw

her two eyes, after I saw her, all activity, all movement became meaningless. The odd thing is that, I don't know why I
always painted the same exact scene on the pen cases. They
were exactly the same. I always drew a cypress tree with a
hunched old man sitting underneath. He was wrapped in a
cape like an Indian yogi and wore a turban on his head. He
had the index finger of his left hand on his lips in a gesture of
surprise. In front of him, a girl wearing a long black dress
was bending down to offer him a water lily. A gentle stream
flowed between them. Had I seen this scene before? Was it a
vision from a dream? I don't know. All I know is that I always painted the same exact scene as if I had no control over
my hand. What's even more strange is that there were always
customers for my pen cases. I would even ship them to my
uncle in India who would sell them and send me the money.

The scene on the pen cases seemed both near and distant.
I really don't remember—but now it's coming back to me. I
said: I must write down my memories, but this incident happened much later and has nothing to do with the story. It
was because of this that I completely stopped painting. It
was two months ago. No, it was two months and four days.
It was the thirteenth day after Nowruz[1] and all the people
had left the city. I had closed my window so I could concen-
trate on my paintings. It was dusk when the door suddenly
opened and in walked my uncle. Well, he said he was my
uncle—I had never seen him before. That's because from the
time he was young he had left on a distant journey. Apparently, he was a ship captain. I had heard he was engaged in
some kind of trade and assumed that's what he wanted with
me. In any case, my uncle was a hunched old man with an
Indian turban on his head and a yellow, tattered cape on his
shoulders, and a scarf wrapped around his head and neck.

His collar was open and you could see his hairy chest. You could count every single whisker on his chin, which stuck out from under his scarf. He had red, infectious eyelids and sugary lips. We bore a distant, laughable resemblance to each other, as if my fevered image had been projected on a distorting mirror. I had always imagined this is what my father would have looked like. As soon as he came in, he went to the corner of the room and crouched. I figured I should offer him something. I went into the dark pantry and looked in every corner to see if I could find something to offer him even though I knew I had nothing—no wine, no opium. Suddenly my eyes caught a small flask on the shelf—it was like a revelation. It was an old flask of aged wine I had inherited. Apparently, it was bottled on the day I was born. It was right there on the shelf. It had never crossed my mind. I had completely forgotten that there is such a thing in the house. I pulled over the stool and stepped up to reach the shelf. But as I reached to take the flask I caught sight of the outside world through the small opening over the shelf. In the field behind my place I saw a hunched old man sitting under a cypress tree with a young woman—no, a celestial angel—in front of him, bending down to offer him a purple water lily with her right hand. The old man was chewing the index finger of his left hand.

The girl was right in front of me but seemed completely unaware of her surroundings. She was looking without seeing. A frozen half smile curled her lip as if she were thinking of someone absent. That's when I saw her frightening, hypnotic eyes. They seemed angry, scolding. They were anxious, curious, and threatening. I felt my life force dissolve in those radiant, defining globes and get sucked into their depths. As much as the human mind can conceive, this seductive mirror drew my entire being toward itself. Her slanted, Turkman eyes were intoxicating, unearthly. They were frightening and seductive at the same time, as if they had witnessed horrifying, supernatural scenes that others can't see. She had prominent cheekbones, a long forehead, thin eyebrows that reached each other, and fleshy, half-open lips—lips that looked as if they had just separated from a long, passionate kiss but remained insatiate. Her black, disheveled hair fell casually around her moonlike face. One strand was glued to her temple. Her soft features, her ethereal figure, and carefree movement spoke of her fleeting, shadowy being. Only a dancer in an Indian temple could move with such elegance. Her gloomy demeanor, her melancholy happiness showed that she was not like ordinary people. Her beauty was unnatural. She struck me like a magical, drug-induced vision.

She lit the fire of the love of a mandrake in me. Her slender figure, the lines of her shoulders, arms, breasts, hips, and legs seemed as if they had just been extracted from the body of her lover—like the female mandrake ripped from the embrace of her mate.

She was wearing a black pleated dress that clung to her body like a mold. As I looked, it seemed as if she wanted to jump over the stream that separated her and the old man but couldn't. Then the old man started to laugh. It was a dry, disturbing laugh that made the hair of your body stand on end. It was a hard, mocking laugh, but his face never changed. It seemed to echo out of some abyss.

Terrified, I jumped off the stool with the flask of wine in my hand—I don't know why I was shaking—it was a kind of tremor full of fear and desire, as if I had just woken from a vivid nightmare. I put the flask of wine on the floor and held my head in my hands. How many minutes, how many hours did I stay like that? I don't know. As soon as I came to, I picked up the flask of wine and went into the room. I saw that my uncle was gone and had left the door open a crack— like the mouth of a cadaver—but the dry laugh of the old man still rang in my ears.

It was getting dark. The lantern was starting to smoke. The intoxicating, terrifying tremor I had felt before was still with me. My life changed from that moment—and all it took was one look, one look from that heavenly angel, that ethereal girl, and as far as the human mind can comprehend, she left her imprint on me.

By this point I was beside myself. I felt like I had known her name before. The glow in her eyes, her smell, her complexion, her movement, it all seemed familiar to me. It was like getting a glimpse of a previous life where my soul neighbored hers. We were of the same origin, built from the same substance. We must have been united. And I must have been close to her in this life. I never wanted to touch her—the invisible ray that emanated from our bodies and drew us together was enough. It was incredible—she seemed familiar to me from first glance. Don't lovers always feel they have known each other before, that a strange relationship has always existed between them? In this degenerate world, I wanted her love or no love at all. Could it be possible that someone would have such an effect on me? But that dry, disturbing laugh of the old man—that sinister laugh tore at the bond between us.

I thought about this all night. A few times I was tempted to go and look through the opening in the wall but I was afraid of the old man's laughter. The next day I was still thinking about this. Could I totally close my eyes to having seen her? The next day, with a thousand trepidations, I decided to put the flask of wine back in its place. But as soon as I pulled aside the curtain to the pantry I saw a black wall in front of me, like the blackness that had consumed my whole life. In fact, there was no opening to the outside. The opening in the corner was completely sealed and had become part of the wall—as if it had never been there in the first place. I fetched the stool but as much as I punched the wall like a madman and listened, as much as I examined it under the light, I couldn't find the slightest trace of the opening. My blows were futile against the thick wall—it had become a wall of lead.

Was it in my power to put this behind me? But I had no control over it. After this I became a tortured soul. No matter how much I waited, how much I searched, it was all in vain. I walked all around the house not for just one day or two days, but for two months and four days. Like a blood-stained killer who returns to the scene of the crime, I circled my house aimlessly every evening at dusk to the point where I got to know every stone, every patch of dirt. But I did not find any sign of the cypress tree, the narrow stream, or the people I had seen there. Every night I knelt before the moon. Maybe she had also looked at the moon. I begged the trees, the stones, all the creatures for help, but did not find any trace of her. Finally, I realized that everything I did was in vain because she could not be attached to the things of this world. The water she used to wash her hair must have come from some mysterious spring or secret cave. Her clothes were not made from ordinary wool, they were not sewn by earthly hands—she was a chosen being. I understood that those water lilies were not ordinary flowers. I was sure that if she put regular water on her face, her face would wilt. And if she picked a normal water lily with her long, delicate fingers, the

skin on her fingers would peel off like petals. I understood
all this. This girl—no, this angel—was a source of wonder
and inspiration for me. Her being was delicate and untouch-
able. She had instilled a sense of worship in me. I was sure
that the glance of a stranger, an ordinary person, would de-
file her and make her wither.

From the time I lost her, from the time when a stone wall,
a dam as heavy as lead without an opening, went up between us, I felt like my life no longer had meaning. Even
though I had enjoyed the most profound pleasure in seeing
her, it was all one-sided because she had not seen me. But I
needed those eyes. Only one look from her was enough to
solve all philosophical problems and divine riddles—one
look from her and there would be no more secrets.

After this, I increased my drink and opium. But alas, instead of dulling my pain and helplessness, instead of making
me forget—day by day, hour by hour, minute by minute—
they made visions of her, her face, her figure, appear more
vividly in front of my eyes.

How could I forget? With eyes closed or open, asleep or
awake, I constantly saw her in front of me. Through the
opening in the pantry—like a ghost that consumes one's
thoughts, one's logic—through the square hole that opened
to the outside, she was always in front of me.

Peace was forbidden me. How could I have any peace? I
got into the habit of going for a walk every evening at dusk.
I don't know why but I was determined to find the stream of
water, the cypress tree, and the bush of water lilies. The
same way I had gotten used to smoking opium, I got used to
these walks—as if a hidden force were pushing me along. The
whole time I thought of her. I thought of the first time I saw
her on the thirteenth day after Nowruz and was determined

to find the place. If only I could find that place. If only I could sit underneath that cypress tree, surely a calm would come over my life. But alas, there was nothing there except rubble and hot stones, and the rotting ribcage of a horse, and a dog sniffing through the trash. Had I really met her? Never! I had only snuck a peak from a hole, from the pathetic opening in the pantry of my place—like a stray dog sniffing through garbage in search of something to eat. The dog runs and hides when they bring out the bins but returns later to search for his own tasty morsels in the fresh trash. I felt the same way, but the opening had been sealed. For me she was a bouquet of fresh flowers that had been thrown on the trash heap.

On that last night, I went for a walk like other nights—it was drizzling and a thick fog blanketed everything. In rainy weather when the brightness is stripped off colors and the impropriety is removed from the silhouettes of objects, I could feel calm and free—as if the rain were washing away my dark thoughts. On that night, the thing that should not have happened, happened. I was prowling aimlessly. But during these hours of solitude, these minutes that I had lost track of, her fading face, as if peeking through cloud or smoke, a face without movement or expression, like the paintings on pen-case covers, appeared before me.

When I returned, I think much of the night had passed and the thick fog had settled so that I could barely see in front of my feet. But I felt an unusual sentience boiling up inside me—when I reached the door, I could sense a body dressed in black, a woman's body, sitting on the front stoop to my house.

I lit a match to find the keyhole, and don't know why I instinctively turned toward her black-clad body. I recognized her eyes. They were the same large, black eyes that radiated like moonlight from her narrow face, the same eyes that stared without seeing. Even if I had never seen them before I still would have recognized them. No—I was not mistaken—this was her black-clad body. Like someone who is dreaming, and knows he is dreaming, and wants to wake up but can't, I just stood there mute and dumb. I was frozen in place. The flame reached the end of the match and burned my fingers. Then I came to. I turned the key and the door opened. I moved to the side. She got up and walked through the dark entrance like someone who knows the way. She opened the door and I walked in behind her. With shaking hands, I lit the lamp; I saw she had gone to my bed and was lying down. Her face was in the shadow. I didn't know if she could see me or not, hear me or not. Apparently, she was neither scared nor had the desire to resist. It was as if she had not come of her own will.

Was she sick? Had she lost her way? Like a sleepwalker, she had not come of her own will. At that moment, no one, no creature could imagine what I went through. I felt this unspeakable, illuminating pain. No! I was not fooled. This was the same woman, the same girl who had calmly walked into my room without saying a word. I had always imagined that our first encounter would be like this. For me, this feeling was like being sentenced to a profound, unending sleep—since one must sink into deep sleep in order to dream such dreams—and this silence was like being sentenced to eternal life, like floating in eternity where one is unable to speak.

For me, she was a woman, but at the same time there was something superhuman about her. Her face made me confused and forget all other faces. I shook as I watched her, my knees buckled—at that moment I saw the entire story of my painful life in her eyes, in her immeasurably large eyes, bright and moist, like two black diamonds that had been dropped in tears. In her eyes, in her black eyes, I found the eternal night and impenetrable darkness I was looking for, and plunged into their horrifying, intoxicating blackness. It felt like all my will had been sucked out of me—the earth shook beneath my feet, and if I had fallen down at that moment, I would have experienced inexpressible delight.

My heart stopped. I held my breath, afraid that if I breathed she would disappear like a cloud or a wisp of smoke. Her silence was a miracle, as if a crystal wall had been erected between us. From that minute, that hour, that moment of eternity, I completely choked. Her tired eyes— like eyes that had seen unnatural things others can't see, like eyes that had seen death—slowly closed. Her eyelids came together. And like a drowning man who after flailing and struggling breaks the surface of the water—I shivered from the burning heat of fever and wiped the sweat from my brow with my sleeve.

Her face still had the same calm and motionless expression but seemed thinner and more sullen—as she lay there, she chewed the nail on her left index finger. Her face was lit by moonlight and through the thin black dress that clung to her body, you could see the outline of her calf, her arm, both sides of her breast, and the entire length of her body.

I bent down to see her better because her eyes were closed, but the more I looked at her, the more distant she seemed. Suddenly, I realized I knew nothing of the secrets of her heart and there was no connection between us—I wanted to say something but was afraid that her ears, her sensitive ears that must have been accustomed to soft, celestial music, would be disgusted by my voice.

It occurred to me that she might be hungry or thirsty. I went into the pantry off my room to find something for her even though I knew I had nothing in the house—but it was like a revelation—on the top shelf, I had a flask of aged wine I had inherited from my father. I brought the stool and took down the flask of wine—I tiptoed next to the bed. I saw that she was sleeping like a tired, worn-out child—she was completely asleep and her long eyelashes rested on each other like velvet. I opened the flask and gently poured a cup of wine into her mouth through her clenched teeth.

When I saw her closed eyes, I felt a sudden calm for the first time in my life, as if the taskmaster who always tortured me and the nightmare that always raked my insides with its metal claws had relaxed a bit. I brought my chair next to the bed and stared at her face—what a childlike face, what an odd expression! Was it possible that this woman, this girl, or this angel of torment—because I didn't know what name to give her—was it possible for her to have a double life, so calm, so carefree? Now I could sense the heat of her body and smell the moist scent that rose from her black, heavy tresses. I don't know why I reached out—I had no control over my hand—and touched her curls, curls that were always glued to her temples. Then I ran my fingers through her hair. It was cold and moist—cold, completely cold—as if she had been dead for days. I wasn't mistaken. She was dead. I reached through the front of her dress and put my hand on her breast and heart—there wasn't the slightest beat. I brought the mirror and held it in front of her nose but there wasn't the slightest sign of life in her.

I wanted to warm her with the heat of my own body, give her my warmth and take the coldness of death from her—maybe this way I could breathe my own soul into her body. I took off my clothes and lay next to her on the bed—we clung to each other like the male and female of the mandrake—her body was just like the body of the female mandrake that's been ripped from the embrace of her mate, and had the same burning love of the mandrake. Her mouth had a bitter, acrid taste, like the butt end of a cucumber; her whole body was as cold as hail. I felt the cold penetrate to the depths of my heart and freeze the blood in my arteries—all my efforts were in vain. I got off the bed and put on my clothes—no, it was no lie—she had come into my room, my bed, and surrendered her body to me. Her body and her soul, she gave both to me!—while she was alive, while her eyes were still full of life—only the memory of her eyes tortured me. But now, senseless, motionless, cold and with closed eyes, she surrendered herself to me—with closed eyes!

This was the same person who had poisoned my entire life. In fact, my life was meant to be poisoned—I could not have any life but a poisoned one. Now, here in my room, she gave me her body and her shadow—her fragile, temporal soul that had no ties to the world of earthlings slowly withdrew from her black pleated dress and the body that tortured her—and joined the world of wandering shadows. Apparently, she took my shadow along with her, but her body, senseless and motionless, was lying there. Her soft, limp muscles, her veins, sinews and bones were waiting to rot, to become a tasty meal for maggots and rats underground. And I, in this room of poverty, full of misery and destitution, a room that seemed like a grave in the midst of the dark, eternal night that blanketed me and pressed into the walls—I had to spend a dark, cold, endless night in the company of a corpse. There was a cold corpse, senseless and motionless in the dark room with me.

In that moment, my mind froze and a strange and new existence welled up inside me—my life was bound to all the living beings around me, all the shadows that shimmered about me. I felt a deep and inseparable connection to the world, to nature, to the movement of creatures—electrifying invisible strands bound me to all the elements of nature. There were no thoughts, no ideas that seemed unnatural to me—I was easily able to unlock the mysteries of ancient paintings, the secrets to impenetrable books of philosophy, the futility of perpetual obstacles—because at this moment I was partaking in the rotation of the earth and planets, the growth of vegetation, and the movement of animals. Past and present, near and far, they attached themselves to me and became associates of my sentient being.

At times such as this, each person falls back on ingrained habits and tested obsessions: the drinker gets drunk, the writer writes, the stone mason chisels, and each soothes the hidden suffering and the burden that weighs down the heart by escaping into the established principles of his life—and it is at times like this that a true artist can create a masterpiece. But I, a helpless and untalented painter of pen-case covers, what could I do? With these dull and soulless images that all looked the same, how could I create a masterpiece? But I felt this overflowing excitement, this overwhelming heat, a special agitation that made me want to paint her eyes on paper—eyes that had closed forever—and keep them for myself. This feeling made me act on my decision, it was no longer in my hands, especially since I was locked up with a corpse—the mere thought of it gave me a strange peace of mind.

Finally, I turned off the smoking lantern and brought two candles and lit them above her head—by candlelight her features seemed softer, and in the subtle shadows of the room they took on a mysterious, ethereal air. I took my pen and paper and went to the side of the bed—the bed that now belonged to her. I wanted to put the lines of her face down on paper, a face condemned, little by little, to decomposition and nothingness. I chose the very lines that had inspired me—no matter how plain or simple a painting is, it needs to be potent, to have a soul. But I, who was used to copying the same image on pen-case covers, now I had to use my brain and try to conjure in my imagination the face that had had such an impact on me—to take one look at her face and then close my eyes and draw the lines of her face on paper. In this way, maybe I could find an opiate for my tortured soul—at last, I took refuge in the motionless lines of images.

The corpse as a subject seemed to have a special affinity with my painting style—painting the dead—I was always a painter of cadavers. But those eyes, her closed eyes, did I need to see them again, were they not sufficiently imprinted on my imagination?

Until close to dawn, I don't know how many times I sketched her face, but I shredded them all—I neither got tired of this nor did I sense the time go by.

It was twilight and a hushed glow seeped into my room through the window. I was busy with a sketch that I thought was better than the others, but her eyes—eyes that seemed to scold as if I had committed an inexcusable sin—I could not bring those eyes on paper. Then, in that moment, the substance, the look of those eyes disappeared from my memory—all my efforts were in vain and as much as I stared at her face, I couldn't remember their expression. Suddenly, I noticed a hint of color creeping back into her cheeks. It was the red color of liver, the color of the meat that hangs outside the butcher shop. She had come to life. Her immeasurably open and surprised eyes—eyes that brimmed with the luster of life but glowed with an unhealthy light—her afflicted, scolding eyes slowly opened and stared at my face. It was the first time she had noticed me—she looked at me and then her eyes closed again. This took no more than an instant but it lasted long enough for me to grasp the essence of her eyes and sketch them on paper—I drew them with the tip of my pen but this time I didn't tear the paper.

Then I got up from where I was sitting and gently approached her. She is alive, I thought, she has come to life, my love has breathed a soul into her body. But from close, I could smell the dead body, the dead and decomposing body—little maggots wriggled on her corpse and two golden bee flies flew around her in the candlelight—she was completely dead. But how, why had her eyes opened? Had I imagined it? Was it real?

I don't want anyone to ask me this, but the heart of the matter was her face—no, it was her eyes, and now I had those eyes. I had the soul of her eyes on paper and had no more use for her body, a body that was condemned to nothingness, fodder for maggots and rats underground. Now she was under my command, not I under hers—now I could see her eyes whenever I pleased. I took the painting and carefully put it in a tin can where I keep my money and hid it in the pantry off my room.

The night, satiated with rest, was sneaking away. One could hear distant, muted sounds, maybe a passing bird was dreaming, maybe plants were growing—at that moment, pale stars disappeared behind stacked clouds. I felt the gentle breath of dawn on my face, and a rooster started to crow from afar.

What could I do with a corpse, a corpse that had started to decompose? At first it crossed my mind to bury her in my own room. Then I thought I would take her out and throw her into a well, a well with purple water lilies growing around it—all this so that no one could see how much thought, how much effort and dexterity this needed! Besides, I didn't want a stranger's eyes to behold her. I had to do everything by myself, with my own hands—the hell with me, my life was meaningless without her. But her, never, never, no ordinary person, no one but me could ever look at her dead body—she had come into my room to surrender her cold body and her shadow to me so that no other person would see her, so that she would not be sullied by the eyes of a stranger. Finally, I had an idea: if I chopped up her body and put her in a suitcase, my same old suitcase, I could take her out with me—far, very far away from people's eyes and bury her.

This time I did not hesitate. I brought the knife with the bone handle that I had in the pantry off my room and very carefully cut the thin black dress that wrapped around her body like a spider's web. I cut the only thing covering her. It was as if she had gotten taller—she seemed taller—then I severed her head. Cold drops of coagulated blood oozed from her throat—then I cut off her arms and legs and fit her trunk and all its parts neatly in the suitcase, and pulled her dress, the same black dress, over her. I locked the lid of the suitcase and put the key in my pocket and breathed a sigh of relief. I weighed the suitcase, it was heavy, I had never felt so tired before—no, I would never be able to carry the suitcase by myself.

The sky clouded over again and it started to drizzle. I left my room; maybe I could find someone to help me with the suitcase—there was no one in sight. But I looked closely and a little farther away, through the fog, I saw a hunched old man sitting under a cypress tree. You could not see his face, which was wrapped in a wide scarf—I slowly went near. I hadn't said a thing when the old man burst into a dry and disturbing laugh, the laugh of a half-breed that made the hair of my body stand on end, and said:

"If you want porter I'm ready, hah—I have hearse-wagon too—every day I take corpse to Shabdolazim² and bury there, hah. I make coffin too, I can make for any size, they are always right size, I'm ready, hah, right now!"

He laughed so hard his shoulders shook. I motioned with my hand toward my house but he didn't give me a chance to talk: "Not necessary, I know your house, right now, hah."

He got up from his seat. I started back toward my house, went in the room and with great effort, dragged the suitcase to the door. I saw an old, dilapidated hearse-wagon by the door. It was tied to two emaciated black nags that looked like corpses. The hunched old man was sitting at the helm holding a long whip in his hand, but he never turned to look at me—with great effort I lifted the suitcase into the wagon and saw a niche carved out for a coffin. I climbed up and lay inside the niche and placed my head on the ledge so I could see out—then I slid the suitcase on my chest and held it tight with both hands.

The whip cracked in the air and the horses set off, panting. You could see their breath, which came out of their nostrils like smoke columns in the rain. They took long, gentle strides—their thin legs trod the ground gingerly, soundlessly, like thieves who according to the law have had their fingers amputated and the stumps dunked in hot oil. The bells around their necks sang a peculiar melody. An inexplicable sense of comfort inundated me, to the extent that I didn't feel the movement of the hearse-wagon—I could only feel the weight of the suitcase on my ribcage.

Her dead body, her corpse—it was as if this weight had always pressed down on my chest. A thick fog covered the road. The wagon crossed mountains, fields and rivers with surprising ease and speed. Around me, I saw novel scenes I had never seen before in dreams or in real life. I saw truncated hills. I saw gray houses in the shape of triangles, cubes and prisms from between cursed, stunted trees that lined both sides of the road. The houses had short, dark, glassless windows—windows that looked like confused eyes, delirious with fever. It seemed like no living creature could possibly live in these houses. Maybe they were built for the shadows of ethereal creatures.

Apparently, the wagoner was taking me on a special path, some backroad lined with the cut torsos of twisted trees through which you could see uneven houses in geometric shapes: cones, retarded cones with slim, crooked windows. Between the houses, purple water lilies climbed the walls. Suddenly, the scene disappeared into a thick fog—heavy, pregnant clouds pressed onto the mountain peaks and the drizzle of rain, like wandering particles, hung in the air. After we had traveled for some time, the hearse-wagon stopped near a barren mountain. I slid the suitcase off my chest and got out.

Beside the mountain there was a calm, lovely area, a place I had never seen before and didn't know about—but it seemed familiar to me, as if it had existed on the fringes of my imagination. The ground was covered with scentless, purple water lilies. I thought no one has ever been to this place. As I placed the suitcase on the ground, the old wagoner turned to me and said, "This place close to Shabdol-azim. You can't find better place. No bird fly here."

I reached into my pocket to pay the wagoner's fare but

only had two qiran and one abasi coins[3]. The wagoner burst
into a dry and disturbing laugh and said, "Don't worry
about it, okay? I will get from you later. I know your house.
You don't need me more, hah? I just want you to know I not
without skill with dig graves, hah. Don't be shy. Let's go
right here, near river next to cypress tree. I will dig ditch for
you right size of suitcase, then will go."

The old man jumped off the wagon with an unusual nimbleness I could not have imagined. I took the suitcase and we
went beside a tree that was next to the dry river.

"This place good," he said.

Without waiting for an answer, he started digging with
the pick and shovel he had with him. I put the suitcase down
and just stood there mesmerized. The old man with the
hunched back and the nimbleness of a seasoned hand was
busy digging. As he dug into the ground, he unearthed something that looked like a glazed, earthen jug. He wrapped it in
a filthy piece of cloth, got up, and said, "Here's ditch, hah.
Exactly size of suitcase, hah."

I reached into my pocket to pay his fare but only had two
qiran and one abasi coins. The old man burst into a dry, disturbing laugh and said:

"Not necessary. It's nothing. I know your house, hah—
and instead of my fare I found earthen jug, it is vase from
Rhages, old city of Rey, hah."

Then he laughed with his twisted, hunched body, so that
his shoulders shook. He put the earthen jug, which he had
wrapped in a filthy cloth under his arm and went toward the
hearse-wagon and climbed to the seat with unusual nimbleness. The whip cracked in the air, the horses set off, panting.
In the misty air, the bells around their necks sang a peculiar
melody. Little by little, they disappeared into the thick fog.

As soon as I was by myself, I breathed a sigh of relief. It was as if a heavy weight had been lifted off my chest and a delightful calm covered me from head to toe. I looked around me. I was in a small area caught between bruised hills and mountains. On one mountain chain you could see remnants of ancient structures of thick mud brick near a dry riverbed—it was a cozy area, remote and quiet. I was happy from the bottom of my heart. I thought to myself when those large eyes open from this earthly sleep they will find a place worthy of their constitution, their beauty—she must stay far from others, far from other corpses, the same way she was far from others when alive.

I carefully lowered the suitcase into the ditch—it was exactly the size of the suitcase, not a hairbreadth's difference. But I wanted to look inside one last time—inside the suitcase. I looked around, not a soul could be seen. I took the key out of my pocket and opened the suitcase. But as I lifted the corner of her black dress, in the middle of the coagulated blood and the wriggling maggots, I saw two large, black, expressionless eyes looking straight at me—my life had drowned in the bottom of these eyes. I quickly closed the suitcase and threw dirt on it and stomped on the dirt until it was packed. I brought some of the purple, scentless water lilies and arranged them on the dirt, then I scattered some rocks and pebbles on it so that no one would be able to find the grave. I did this so well that even I couldn't make out the grave from the rest of the ground around it.

When I finished, I looked at myself. I saw my clothes were torn, covered in dirt, and had black, coagulated blood pasted on them—two golden bee flies were flying around me and little maggots were stuck to my body. They were squirming against one another. I wanted to clean the blood from my clothes. I wet my sleeve with spit but the more I rubbed the stain the more it spread and got thicker until it covered my whole body—I felt the slimy chill of the blood all over my body.

It was almost dusk and it was drizzling. I started following the tracks of the hearse-wagon without knowing what I'm doing, but I lost the trail as it got dark. With no destination, no thought, no will, I slowly walked in the dense darkness and had no idea where I would end up. I walked along in the dark night, in the bottomless night that had shrouded my entire life. I had seen those large eyes circled by coagulated blood. Now the light housed in those two eyes had been extinguished forever and it made no difference to me if I reached some shelter or not.

Utter silence reigned and I thought everyone had abandoned me. I sought refuge in inanimate objects. I had tapped into the flow of nature, into the profound darkness that had descended on my soul. This silence is a kind of language we don't understand—the intensity of delight made my head spin, I felt nauseous and my legs went numb. I felt infinitely exhausted within. I walked on the burial ground by the road and sat on one of the gravestones. I took my head in my hands, dumbfounded at my own condition—suddenly, the sound of a dry, disturbing laugh made me come to. I turned and saw someone sitting next to me. His head and face were covered in a scarf and he held something wrapped in cloth under his arm. He turned to me and said:

"You probably wanted go to town but lost the way, hah? You probably ask yourself what I'm doing in the graveyard this time of night—but don't be feared, my business is only

with the dead, my job is digging graves, it's not a bad job,
hah? I know all the paths and ditches here—for example,
today I went to dig grave and found this vase under the
dirt, you know, it's from Rhages, it's from old city of Rey,
hah! It's really nothing, I give this jug to you, for you to remember me."

I reached into my pocket and took out two qiran and one
abasi coins. The old man laughed a dry, blood curdling
laugh and said:

"No, never, it's nothing, I know you, and I know your
house—I have hearse-wagon right here. Come on, I drop
you off at your house, hah—it's only two steps away."

He put the earthen jug in my lap and got up—he laughed
so hard his shoulders shook. I took the earthen jug and
started to follow the hunched figure of the old man. Around
the bend in the road there stood a decrepit hearse-wagon
with two emaciated black nags—the old man climbed onto
the seat with unusual nimbleness. I went in and lay down inside the special niche built for a casket and rested my head
on the ledge so I could see around me. I placed the earthen
jug on my chest and held it with my hands.

The whip cracked in the air and the horses set off, panting.
They took long, gentle strides—their legs trod the ground
gingerly, silently. In the misty air, the bells around their necks
sang a peculiar melody—from behind the clouds, the stars
looked down upon the earth like bright eyes bulging out of
their sockets in a pool of black, coagulated blood. A delightful calm covered me from head to toe—only the weight of
the vase, like a dead body, pressed down on my chest. Twisted
trees with crooked branches seemed to be holding one another by the hand as if they were afraid of tripping and

falling over. The road was lined by the truncated, geometric shapes of strange houses with black, deserted windows, but the walls of these houses, like glowworms, radiated with a dull, malignant light. Spray by spray, row by row, the menacing line of trees slipped by—they were running away from one another, but it seemed like the stems of water lilies had wrapped around their legs and was making them fall. My entire life was besieged by the smell of death, the smell of decomposing flesh. Apparently, the smell of death had always penetrated my body and I had spent my entire life lying inside a black casket and a hunched old man whose face I could not see was ushering me through fog and fleeting shadows.

The hearse-wagon stopped and I took the earthen jug and jumped off. I was by the front door of my house. I rushed in, put the earthen jug on the table and fetched the tin can, the same tin can that was my piggy bank, which I kept hidden in the pantry off my room. I went to the door to give it to the old wagoner instead of his fare, but he had disappeared—there was no sign of the old man and his wagon. Disappointed, I returned to my room, turned on the light, removed the earthen jug from its cloth wrapping, and wiped away the dirt with my sleeve. It had a violet glaze, ancient and clear, the color of ground golden bee flies. On one side, purple water lilies lined an almond-shaped frame and in the middle of that . . .

Inside the almond-shaped frame was a drawing of her face, the face of a woman with large, black eyes, larger than usual. They were scolding eyes as if I had committed unforgivable sins I did not know about. They were frightening, bewitching eyes, at the same time restless and surprised, threatening and seductive. The eyes frightened and seduced, and an intoxicating, supernatural glow burned at their core. She had prominent cheekbones, a long forehead, thin eyebrows that reached each other, fleshy, half-open lips, and disheveled hair with one strand glued to her temple.

I took out the portrait I had sketched the night before from the tin can and compared it to the image on the earthen jug—there was no difference, as if they were copies of each other. Both were the same, in fact both were the work of the same person, a pathetic painter of pen-case covers—maybe the soul of the painter of the earthen jug had penetrated me when I was painting and my hand was under his control. You couldn't tell them apart. The only difference was that my painting was on paper whereas the painting on the earthen jug had a bright, antique glaze that gave the image a mysterious soul, an alien, unusual soul—the glint of a mischievous soul sparked from the depths of her eyes. No, it was unbelievable, those were the same, large, distracted eyes, the same reserved look, but at the same time free! No one can fathom how I felt. I wanted to run from myself—was such a thing possible? All the miseries of my life appeared before my eyes again. Were the eyes of one person in my life not enough? Now two people with those eyes, the eyes that belonged to her, were looking at me! No, it was completely insufferable—eyes that had been buried right there near the mountain, beside a cypress tree next to a dry river. These eyes that had been buried underneath purple water lilies in a pool of viscous blood surrounded by worms and venomous creatures reveling around her, among the roots of plants that would soon sink into their sockets and suck out their marrow, now alive and vibrant, were staring at me.

I had never imagined myself to be cursed and miserable to this extent. But despite the awareness of the crime that was hidden inside me, I was struck by this inexplicable, unfamiliar thrill. Because now I understood that I had an old partner in sorrow—was this ancient painter, a painter who had painted this earthen jug hundreds, maybe thousands of years ago, was he not my partner in sorrow? Had he not gone through the same trials as me? Until this moment I had considered myself the most miserable creature in the world. Now I realized that in the rubble of those villages and ponderous brick houses built on the mountain, people had lived whose bones were now putrefied, and bits and pieces of their bodies endured in purple water lilies. Among these people, maybe there existed one cursed painter, one blighted painter, a pathetic maker of pen cases, just like me. Now, I realized, I was able to understand that he too had burned and melted away in the midst of two large, black eyes, just like me—this consoled me.

Finally, I put my painting next to the painting on the earthen jug, then went and prepared my special brazier. When the coals started to glow red I brought them next to the paintings—I took a few hits from the opium pipe and stared at the images in a state of ecstasy—I wanted to gather my thoughts, and only the mysterious smoke of opium could bring my thoughts together and give me peace of mind.

I smoked all the opium I had left so that this strange drug would disperse all my miseries and remove the veil that had covered my eyes—all the piled-up, distant, ashen memories. The feeling I was waiting for came upon me and it was stronger than I had expected—little by little, I sank into a state hovering between sleep and coma—my thoughts became precise, grand, magical.

Then it was as if the pressure, the weight on my chest had been lifted and the laws of gravity no longer applied to me and I was free to take flight with my reveries, which had become

massive, delicate, penetrating—a profound, inexpressible sat-
isfaction inundated my entire being. I was released from the
weight chained to my body. My whole existence leaned toward the slow, numb, vegetative world—a calm world but full
of shapes and bright, magical hues. Then the trail of my
thoughts broke apart and dissolved into patterns and colors—
I was tossed in ethereal waves. I could hear my heartbeat, feel
the blood moving through my arteries—for me, this sensation
was full of meaning, full of bliss.

From the bottom of my heart I wished to surrender myself
to the sleep of oblivion, if such oblivion was possible, if only
it could last—if only I could close my eyes to enter the realm
of nonexistence, beyond gentle sleep, and no longer feel my
own being—if only my entire substance could dissolve in
one ink stain, one melody, or one stroke of color. Then these
waves and shapes would spread so wide and become so huge
that I would completely disappear—then my wish would be
granted.

Little by little, a feeling of numbness and languor crept
over me, a welcome lethargy, a subtle surge that radiated
from my body. Then I felt like my life was moving in
reverse—by degree, I pictured incidents from my past, feelings, erased and long-forgotten childhood memories. Not
only was I seeing them, I was participating in them, I could
feel them—with every passing moment I was becoming
younger, smaller. Then, suddenly my thoughts disbanded
and became dark. I felt like I was hanging from a hook, dan-
gling in the pits of a deep, dark well—then I fell from the
hook. I was sliding deeper, farther, and there was nothing to
break my fall—it was an endless cliff in an eternal night.
Then, one after another, erased scenes materialized before
my eyes. I passed through a moment of absolute oblivion—

when I came to, I found myself in a small room—it seemed
unfamiliar but at the same time natural.

———————

I woke up in a new world but it all seemed very familiar to
me, so familiar that I felt a stronger attachment to it than to
my old life—as if it were a reflection of my real existence. It
was a different world but seemed closer, more pertinent, as if
I had returned to my original environment—I had been reborn into an ancient world but one closer and more natural.

It was still twilight. The light from a tallow-burning lamp
was flickering from the shelf in my room; there was a mat-
tress in the corner but I was awake. My body felt hot and
there were bloodstains on my cloak and scarf, and my hands
were covered in blood. But even with the fever and dizziness,
I felt an odd excitement—stronger than the thought of getting rid of the bloodstains, stronger than the fear of being
arrested by the sheriff. In any case, I had expected to fall into
the hands of the sheriff for some time now, but planned to
down a whole cup of the poisoned wine before being arrested. The need to write had become an obsession, a duty—
I wanted to expel the demon that had been raking at my
entrails for so long. I wanted to broadcast my bravery by
putting it all down on paper.

Finally, after some moments of hesitation, I drew the
tallow-burning lamp near and started like this:

———————

"I have always thought it best to remain extinguished, to
spread one's wings like a bird and sit by the sea in solitude.

But now it is no longer in my hands because the thing that should not have happened, happened—who knows, maybe right at this moment, or in an hour, a band of drunken patrolmen will come to arrest me—I have no interest in saving my carcass, besides, it's already too late. Let's assume I do get rid of the bloodstains—before they get their hands on me I will drink a cup of that wine, the wine that is my birthright, which I keep on the shelf.

"Now I want to crush my entire life in the palm of my hand like a bunch of grapes, and pour its extract, no, its wine—like holy water from Karbala—drop by drop into the parched throat of my shadow. But before I go, I want to put down on paper the pain that, little by little, has been eating away at me in the corner of this room like termites in an open wound—easier this way to organize my thoughts. Do I intend to write a will? Never. I neither have any property that the court can consume, nor any faith that the devil can walk away with. What in this world could possibly have the least bit of value for me—I have already lost everything in life. I have let it all slip away, and after I'm gone, I don't give a damn if anyone reads my shredded pieces of paper or not. I am only writing out of necessity, out of a sudden need. I need more than ever to connect my thoughts to my own imaginary self, my shadow—this sinister shadow hunched on the wall by the light of the tallow-burning lamp, that appears to read carefully and consume whatever I write. This shadow must know better than me! I can speak freely only with my own shadow; he's the one who makes me talk; he's the only one who truly knows me; he must understand . . . I want to pour the extract, no, the bitter wine of my existence, drop by drop into the parched throat of my shadow and say, 'This is my life!'

"If anyone saw me yesterday, they would have seen a broken, sickly young man, but today they will see a hunched old man with white hair, hollow eyes, and sugary lips. I'm afraid to look out my window, to look at myself in the mirror, because I see my own twin shadow everywhere. But in order to describe my life to my bent shadow, I have to recount a story—alas, there are so many tales of childhood, love, sex, weddings, death, and none are true—I'm tired of narratives and fabrications.

"I will try to crush these grapes. But will there be the least bit of truth in it? I really don't know. I don't know where I am, don't know if the patch of sky above my head or this plot of earth I'm sitting on belongs to Nishapur, Balkh, or Benares—I'm not sure of anything.

"I have seen so many contradictory things, heard so many differing accounts—my outlook has been so grated by the facade of objects. From behind this thin, obstinate veil that conceals the soul, I don't believe anything. I doubt the weight and firmness of objects, the clear and evident truths of the present. I don't know, if I were to strike the stone mortar in the corner of the yard with my fingers and ask it if it is solid and stable, would I believe its affirmative response or not?

"Am I not a singularly distinct creature? I don't know. But now, when I look in the mirror, I don't recognize myself—that former 'me' is dead, dead and decomposed—but there is no barrier between us. I have to tell my story, but I don't know where to start—life is a series of anecdotes, from end to end. I must crush the bunch of grapes and pour their extract, spoonful by spoonful, into the parched throat of my shadow.

"Where should I start? The thoughts that are boiling up in my head right now belong to this moment, they have no date and time—one incident from yesterday might be older and more distant to me that an incident from a thousand years ago.

"Maybe since I cut all ties to the world of the living, old memories are reappearing before my eyes—past, future, hour, day, month, year—they are all the same to me. The different stages of childhood, youth, or old age are nothing but hollow conceptions. They have veracity only for ordinary people, for the vulgar—emphasis on *vulgar*, that's the word I was looking for—for the vulgar whose lives have seasons and well-defined parameters, like the seasons of the year in temperate climates. But my entire life has unfolded in the same way, in the same season—as if I have lived my entire life in a frigid climate, in endless darkness—whereas a flame has always burned at my core, which has made me melt like a candle.

"Like a candle that melts away little by little, my life was melting away inside the four walls of my room, inside the fortress I had erected around my life and my thoughts. But no, I'm mistaken—my life was more like a wet log lying in the corner of the fireplace that turns into hot coal from the fire of the other logs but neither burns nor remains wet and fresh—it only suffocates from the smoke of others. My room, like all other rooms, is built with brick and mortar on the ruins of thousands of older houses. It has whitewashed walls and a frieze—just like a tomb. The smallest detail of the room will occupy my thoughts for hours, like a little spider in the corner of the wall—because since I've been bedridden, they attend to me less often. A child's crib that was used for me and my wife still hangs from the large nail in the wall—maybe it had also held the weight of other children. Just below the nail there is a board on the wall that is peeling back. From underneath it I can smell the objects and creatures that had been in this room before me, to such an extent that no current of fresh air, no wind has been able to remove their thick, lazy, stubborn stench from the room—the smell of sweat, the smell of ancient diseases, the odor of mouths and feet, the sharp smell of urine, the smell of stale oil, rotten straw, burnt eggs, the smell of fried onions, decoctions, the smell of a baby's regurgitations and pacifiers, the smell of a boy's room who has just reached puberty, vapors from the street, the smell of the dead and those still alive but on their deathbed, and other smells that have left their trace but whose source is unclear.

"My room has a dark pantry and two openings to the outside, to the world of the vulgar. One opens up onto our own yard and the other faces the street and connects me to the city of Rey—a city described as the bride of the earth with its winding alleys, down-pressed homes, schools, and caravanserais. Rey, considered the largest city in the world, lives and breathes right outside my room. Here in the corner of my room, when I close my eyes, I can see the faint shadows of the city, its kiosks, its mosques, its gardens, and all the things that have left their mark on me.

"These two openings connect me to the outside world, to the world of the vulgar. But in my room, there is also a mirror on the wall in which I see my own face—in my cramped life, this mirror is more important than the world of the vulgar, which has nothing to do with me.

"From all the scenes in this city, the one in front of the opening in my room is of a humble butcher shop that consumes two sheep every day. When I look out, I see the butcher. Every morning, two emaciated black nags, consumptive nags with a deep, dry cough and stiff legs that terminate in hooves—as if they had been amputated according to some primitive law and dunked in hot oil—carry the carcasses of four sheep to the shop. The butcher rubs his greasy hands on his hennaed beard. First, he looks the carcasses up and down with the eyes of a buyer, chooses two of them, and weighs the tail fat with his hand, then hangs them on hooks outside his shop. The horses set off, panting. Then the butcher caresses the bloody corpses with their cut throats, their bulging eyes, and bloodstained eyelids that protrude from their bruised skulls—he feels them up. Then he takes a bone-handled knife and cuts them up very carefully and sells the meat to his customers with a smile. He does everything with such delight! I am sure he gets immense pleasure out of it. That yellow dog with the thick neck, which has staked out our neighborhood—the one with the bent head and innocent eyes—stares at the butcher's hands with envy. The dog also knows all this, knows that the butcher enjoys his job.

"A little farther, a strange old man sits under an awning with all kinds of wares laid out in front of him. On his spread there is a sickle, two horseshoes, a few colorful beads, a knife, a mousetrap, a rusty pair of pliers, a bottle of ink, a comb with broken teeth, a small shovel, and a glazed, earthen jug, which he has covered with a filthy piece of cloth. I have watched him for hours, days, months. He sits there always in the same position with his dirty scarf, his camel-colored cloak, his open collar through which his white chest hair sticks out, his afflicted eyelids that swallow the malady and impropriety of his stubborn look, and the talisman tied around his arm. On Friday nights, with his yellowed, half-broken teeth, he recites the Koran. Apparently, that's how he makes his living because I never see anyone buy anything from him—his face is the face I usually see in my nightmares. I wonder what stubborn and stupid thoughts, like foul weeds, run through his round, shaved head, his short forehead wrapped inside the cream-colored turban. Apparently, the spread in front of the old man and all the junk on it has a special relation to his life. A couple of times, I decided to go talk to him or buy something from him, but I didn't have the courage.

"My wet nurse told me that the man was a potter in his youth and had only kept that one earthen jug for himself. Now, he makes his living by peddling.

"These are my connections to the outside world, but in my domestic life, all I have left is my old wet nurse and my slut wife. But Naneh-joon was also her wet nurse—not only are my wife and I close relatives, Naneh-joon nursed both of us at the same time. My wife's mother was practically my mother. I never met my parents, and her mother, that regal woman with the gray hair, raised me. It was my wife's mother who I loved like my own mother—it was my affection for her that made me marry her daughter.

"I have heard a number of different stories about my parents. Only one of these stories, the one Naneh-joon told, seems true to me. She told me that my father and uncle were twin brothers. They looked identical, they acted the same, even their voices sounded the same, to the point that it was difficult to tell them apart. They even had a spiritual connection, a mutual, physical empathy where if one got sick, the other would get sick as well. They were, as the expression goes, two halves of an apple. Finally, they both took up trade and at the age of twenty moved to India where they would import and sell handicrafts from Rey, things like different kinds of cloth, cotton cloths with ornate stitching, cloths with flower prints, boxes, scarves, needles, earthen dishes, shampoo, and pen cases. My father was stationed at their base in Benares and my uncle would travel to other cities and sell their goods. After a while, my father fell in love with a virgin, Bugam Dasi, who was a temple dancer of Lingam Puja. Her job was to dance in front of the great statue of Lingam and attend to it—she was a warm-blooded girl with olive skin; lemon breasts; large, slanted eyes; and thin, connecting eyebrows with a red dot in the middle.

"I can imagine Bugam Dasi, my mother, wearing a silk sari with gold stitching, an open shirt and a brocade headband, with her black, heavy tresses, dark as an eternal night, tied in a knot behind her head. She had bracelets on her wrists and ankles; a gold ring through her nostril; large, black, slanted, half-drunken eyes; and bright teeth. She danced with slow, rhythmic movements to the sound of the sitar, tonbak, tanpura, sanj, and karna. It was a gentle, steady song played by naked men wearing turbans—a profound song that expressed all the magic, superstition, lust and pain of the Indians. With elegant swaying and seductive gestures—sacred movements—Bugam Dasi would unfurl her petals and open like a bud, send a shudder along her shoulders and down her arms, then bend low and draw in her petals again. I can just imagine what effect these movements, which conveyed a special meaning and spoke without speaking, would have had on my father. In particular, the rancid, peppery smell of her sweat mixed with jasmine perfume and sandalwood oil would have intensified the erotic atmosphere—perfume that smelled of the sap of exotic trees and gave life to distant, stifled feelings, perfume that smelled of little boxes of medicine, medicine from India that they used to keep in a child's room, and unknown oils from a country full of meaning, full of ancient rights and practices. I guess it was the smell of my childhood decoctions—all these awakened the distant, slaughtered memories of my father, who was so taken by Bugam Dasi that he converted to the dancer's religion and became a worshipper of Lingam. But after a while, the girl became pregnant and was dismissed from her duties at the temple.

"I had just been born when my uncle returned to Benares from one of his trips. Apparently, my uncle, whose tastes and desires were just like my father's, fell head over heels in love with my mother. Finally, he tricked her, an easy task considering the physical and spiritual similarities between him and my father. But soon, my mother discovered their trick and threatened to leave them both unless they agreed to take the test of the cobra[4]—she would belong to the one who survived.

"The test was like this: my father and uncle would be locked inside a dark room, a room like a dungeon, with a cobra. Whoever was bitten would naturally scream, at which point the snake charmer would open the door and rescue the other one, and Bugam Dasi would belong to him.

"Before they were thrown into the dungeon, my father asked Bugam Dasi to dance for him one more time, to dance the sacred dance of the temple. Bugam Dasi agreed and danced in torchlight to the song of the snake charmer's flute, with smooth, rhythmic movements that were full of meaning— with the twists and sways of a cobra. Then they locked my father and uncle into the room with the cobra. But instead of a scream of fear, there arose an odd moan mixed with a disturbing laugh—and then a hideous scream. When they opened the door, it was my uncle who came out—but his face had turned old and broken. My uncle emerged from the horror in that room—the sound of the slithering, hissing snake, its round, glowing eyes, its poisonous fangs and black body, its long neck and large head, wide like a ladle—with white hair. According to the deal, Bugam Dasi now belonged to my uncle—but the terrible thing was that it was not clear who had survived the trial, my father or my uncle. The trial had deranged the survivor, he completely forgot his old life and did not recognize the baby—that is why they thought he was my uncle. Is this story not pertinent to my life? Has the echo of this disturbing laugh, the horror of this trial, not left its mark on me? After that, I was nothing more than an extra mouth to feed. Finally, my uncle or my father and Bugam Dasi returned to Rey for business and entrusted me to his sister, my aunt.

"My wet nurse said that when they were saying goodbye, my mother gave a flask of wine to my aunt. It was wine mixed with the venom of the cobra—what better thing could Bugam Dasi have left as a keepsake for her child? This violet wine, this elixir of death that could grant eternal peace—maybe she had also crushed her life like a bunch of grapes and left the wine to me. This was the same venom that had killed my father—now I realize what a valuable gift she had given me.

"Is my mother still alive? Maybe right now as I am writing, she is in a faraway city in India, twisting and swaying like a snake as she dances in torchlight—as if a cobra has bitten her—surrounded by curious women and children and naked men, with my uncle and his white hair crouching next to the scene and watching, and remembering the dungeon, the slithering hiss of the angry snake with glowing eyes that lifts its neck to reveal a dark-gray line on the back, its head like a ladle.

"In any case, I was just a suckling baby when they put me in Naneh-joon's lap, this same Naneh-joon who was also the wet nurse of my cousin, my slut wife. I was raised by my aunt, that regal woman with the gray hair covering her forehead—I was raised in this same house along with her daughter, this same slut. From the first time I was aware of myself, I looked at my aunt as a mother and loved her. I loved her so much that I took her daughter, my own milk-sister, who later looked so much like her mother, as my wife.

"Was I forced to marry her? She surrendered herself to me only once—I will never forget it—at her mother's deathbed. It was late into the night and most of the household had already gone to sleep. I was in my pajamas and went into the dead woman's room to say a final farewell. Two camphor candles were burning above her head and they had put a Koran on her stomach to stop the devil from entering her body. When I removed the shroud covering her face I saw the dignified, arresting look of my aunt, as if all earthly attractions had been dissolved in her face. I felt the urge to prostrate before her, but at the same time, death seemed so natural to me. There was a mocking smile frozen on the corners of her lips. I wanted to kiss her hand and leave the room, but as I turned, to my surprise, I saw the slut that is now my wife enter the room. Right there in front of the corpse of her mother, she grabbed me with burning passion, pulled me toward her, and covered me in wet kisses! I was so embarrassed I wanted to melt into the ground but didn't know what to do. It seemed like the dead woman with her buck teeth was mocking us—I thought the whole feel of her soft smile had changed. Without realizing what I'm doing, I embraced her and kissed her. At that very moment, the curtain to the adjacent room opened and my aunt's husband, the father of this very same slut, hunched and wrapped in a scarf, entered the room. He laughed a dry, bloodcurdling laugh that shook his shoulders and made the hair of your body stand on end, but he didn't look in our direction. I was so embarrassed I wanted to melt into the ground and if I could have, I would have slapped the dead woman in the face so that she would stop staring at us with that mocking look. Oh, the indignity! Terrified, I ran out of the room—all for the sake of this same slut—maybe she had arranged the whole thing so that I would have to marry her.

"Even though we were practically brother and sister, I had to marry her so their reputation would not get ruined—because she was not a virgin, which I didn't know. How could I have known—but it had reached my ear. The night of our wedding, as much as I pleaded, she did not give in and take her clothes off. She kept saying, 'It's an unclean time for me,' and would not even let me near her. She turned off the light and went and slept on the other side of the room. She was shaking like a leaf, as if she had been thrown into a pit with a dragon. No one will believe me—in fact it is unbelievable—she didn't even let me give her one kiss on the lips. The second night too, I went and slept in the same place as the first night, and the following nights were all the same—I did not dare. Time passed and every night I slept on the floor, on the other side of the room—who would believe me? Two months, no—for two months and four days I slept on the floor, far from her, and did not dare approach her.

"She had prepared that telling rag beforehand, put the blood of a pigeon on it. I don't know, maybe it was the same rag she had kept from the first night she made love—just to ridicule me even more. Then everyone was congratulating me, winking at one another and probably saying to them-

selves: 'That guy sure stormed the castle last night!' And I
said nothing. They were laughing at me, laughing at my
stupidity—I promised myself that one day I would write all
this down.

"Then I found out she had fornicators left and right.
Maybe she hated me because some preacher had recited a
few verses in Arabic that put her under my control—maybe
she wanted to be free. Finally, one night I decided to force
myself on her, and I acted on my decision. But after a furious
struggle she got up and left. That night I satisfied myself in
her bed—I slept and rolled around in her bed, which still
held the heat and scent of her body—that was the only night
I slept peacefully. From that night on, she slept in a separate
room.

"At night, when I came home, she was still not there—I
didn't know if she had come back or not—I didn't want to
know. I was condemned to solitude, condemned to death. I
wanted to make contact with her fornicators however I
could—no one is going to believe this one. I would stalk
whoever I heard she liked. I would humble myself, demean
myself just to meet him—I would flatter him, sweet-talk
him, and bring him for her. And what fornicators: a tripe
seller, a jurisprudent, a liver vendor, the manager of a drug-
store, a theologian, a merchant, a philosopher. Their names
and labels were different, but they were all on par with the
apprentice to the guy who boils lamb's heads—she preferred
all of them to me. No one will believe with what shame and
contempt I belittled myself. I was afraid of losing my wife, so
I tried to learn how to act, how to behave, how to seduce
from her fornicators. But I was just a miserable pimp and all
the idiots were laughing at me—how could I learn the be-
havior and habit of the vulgar? Now I know, she liked them

because they were shameless, stupid, foul—her love was mingled with filth and death. Did I really want to sleep with her? Was I obsessed by the beauty of her face or her hatred of me—maybe it was her movements, her flirtations, or the fondness and love I had for her mother ever since I was a child? Maybe it was all of these together? No, I don't know. I only know one thing: I don't know what kind of poison this woman, this slut, this witch had poured into my soul, that I only wanted her—every atom in my body needed every atom in her body, they were screaming with lust. I desperately wished to be alone with her on a deserted island where no other human being exists. I wished that an earthquake, a storm, or a strike of lightning would destroy all the vulgar who were breathing, running about and enjoying themselves behind the walls of my room, so that only the two of us remained. Would she still prefer any other creature, an Indian serpent or a dragon, to me? I wished to spend one night together with her, and then die in each other's arms. I thought this would be the supreme outcome of my existence.

"It was as if this slut got pleasure out of torturing me, as if the pain that already ate away at me was not enough. Eventually, I ceased all activity and confined myself to the house. I was like a moving corpse, but no one knew the secret between us. My old wet nurse, who was witness to my gradual death, chided me behind my back—all for the sake of this slut. I could hear people whisper to one another, 'How can this poor woman tolerate that crazy husband?' They were right, I had become so loathsome it was hard to believe.

"Day by day I wasted away. When I looked at myself in the mirror, my cheeks had turned red, the color of the meat that hangs outside the butcher shop. My body burned and my eyes looked vacant and sad—I really enjoyed my new

condition and saw the mist of death in my eyes—I knew it
was time to go.

"Finally, they called for the revered physician, the physician to the vulgar, the family physician who according to
himself had raised us. He showed up sporting a beige turban
and a three-span beard. He was proud of having given viril-
ity medication to my grandfather, poured sweet rocket-seed
potion down my throat, and administered purging cassia to
my aunt. As soon as he came in, he sat by my bed, took my
blood pressure and examined my tongue. He ordered me to
drink ass's milk with ground pine, and inhale frankincense
and arsenic vapor twice a day. He also gave this exalted pre-
scription to my wet nurse, which included all kinds of strange
decoctions and oils like hyssop, olive, licorice extract, camphor, maidenhair fern, chamomile oil, gander oil, linseed,
spruce seed, and other nonsense.

"My condition deteriorated. Only my wet nurse, who was
also her wet nurse, would sit in the corner of my room by my
bed, with her old face and gray hair, and put cold water on
my forehead and make me decoctions. She would tell me
about our childhood—mine and that slut's. She told me that
ever since she was in the cradle, my wife had a habit of chewing the nail of her left hand, to the extent that she would lac-
erate herself. And sometimes she would tell me stories. I felt
like these stories were taking me back in time and making
me feel like a child again—they brought back memories of
those days. She would tell me the same stories from when I
was very young and slept in the crib next to my wife—it was
a big two-person crib. Parts of these stories that I never used
to believe before now seemed so real to me, because my illness had given birth to a new world, a faded, alien world full
of images and colors and desires that one cannot imagine

when healthy. I felt the details of these fables with unspeakable delight and excitement—I felt like I had become a child and even now as I write, I feel I am a participant in them. All these feelings belong to this moment, not the past.

"Apparently, the wishes and habits of the ancients had been transferred to subsequent generations through these fables and had become the necessities of life. For thousands of years they have said the same things, had sex the same way, had the same childish problems—is life not a ridiculous story, an unbelievable fable from end to end? Am I not writing my own story, my own fairy tale? Stories are only a way of escaping unrequited desires, unattainable wishes, wishes that any fable-writer has imagined according to his own narrow, inherited nature.

"I wish I could sleep gently the way I used to when I was a child and didn't know anything—a calm, undisturbed sleep. I used to wake up with rosy cheeks, the color of the meat that hangs outside the butcher shop. My body was hot and I was coughing—what deep, frightening coughs. I don't know from what lost gorge in my body they were emanating—like the coughs of the nags that carried lamb carcasses to the butcher early in the morning.

"I totally remember—it was completely dark and for a few minutes I drifted into a coma. Before I fell asleep, I was talking to myself—I was sure that I had become a child and was lying in the crib. I felt someone near me, but it had been some time since the rest of the household had gone to bed. It was close to daybreak—the ill know that this is the time when life extends beyond the boundaries of the earth. My heart was racing but I was not afraid. My eyes were open but I could not see anyone because the darkness was impenetrable. A few minutes passed and a sick thought occurred to me. 'Maybe it's her,' I said to myself—then I felt a cool hand on my burning forehead. I was shaking. Was that not the hand of the Angel of Death? Then I fell asleep. When I woke up in the morning, my wet nurse said it was her daughter (she meant my wife, that slut) who had come to my bedside and cradled my head in her lap and rocked me like a child— apparently a motherly instinct had been awakened in her. I wish I had died at that moment—maybe the child she was pregnant with had died. Had she given birth? I didn't know.

"In this room that kept getting smaller and darker than a grave, I was constantly on the lookout for my wife, but she never came. Was it not because of her that I was in this condition? It was no joke. It was three years, no, two years and four months—but what are days and months? They have no meaning for me—for someone who is in the grave, time loses all meaning. This room was a tomb for me and my thoughts. All the activity, the sounds, the postures of other people's lives—the lives of the vulgar, who are physically and spiritually the same—had become strange and meaningless to me. From the time I became bedridden, I had awakened to an alien, incomprehensible world where I had no need for the world of the vulgar. There was a world inside me, a world full of mysteries where I was forced to explore all its corners and recesses.

"At night, as my soul wavered on the brink between two worlds, just before plunging into the fathomless chasm of sleep, I would dream. In the blink of an eye I was living a life not my own—I was far away, breathing a different air. It was as if I wanted to flee from myself and change my fate. With eyes closed, my real life appeared before me—odd scenes that easily disappeared and appeared again, as if my will had no impact on them. But even this was uncertain. The images that conjured in front of me were not from an ordinary dream because I had not fallen asleep yet. In utter calm and quiet, I separated the images from one another and compared them. Apparently, I had not known myself until this moment. The world as I had known it until now had lost all meaning, all vitality. In its place, a dark night reigned—because they had never taught me to see the night and love the night.

"At that moment, I don't know if I had control over my arms or not. I assumed if I were to leave my hands to their own design, they would act according to some unknown machination all their own, without any intrusion or restraint from me. If I let my guard down and didn't watch over my whole body constantly, it would have been capable of deeds I never expected. This sensation had appeared in me a long time ago and was eating me alive. Not only my body, but my soul was always in conflict with my heart—they could not get along. I was constantly experiencing a kind of alien dissolution and decomposition—I would think of things I could not believe. Despite being reproved by my reason, sometimes a sense of pity would well up in me. Often, I would get into a conversation with someone but my attention would drift. I would think about other things and reproached myself in my heart—I was a decomposing mass. Apparently, I had always been and always would be like that—an odd, unbalanced concoction . . .

"The unbearable thing is that I felt distant from the people I saw and among whom I lived, but we had a superficial resemblance, a resemblance at the same time distant and near that connected me to them. It was the shared necessities of life that assuaged my bewilderment. The resemblance that tortured me most was that the vulgar were also attracted to

this slut, my wife, and she was more inclined toward them—
I am positive that there was a defect in one of us.

"I called her 'slut' because no other name suited her so
well. I don't want to call her 'my wife' because there was no
husband-and-wife allowance between us—I would be lying
to myself. I have always called her slut—the name had special resonance. If I married her it was because she's the one
who took the first step toward me—even though it was just
a ruse. No, she had no interest in me at all—how could she
be interested in anyone? She was a licentious woman who
needed one man for sex, another for making love, and a
third to torture. I doubt she was even content with this trin-
ity, but she had definitely chosen me as the one to be
tortured—in reality, she couldn't have chosen any better. But
I married her because she looked like her mother, because
she had a distant resemblance to me. Now, not only did I
love her, all the atoms in my body desired her, especially in
my loins. I don't want to conceal real emotions under the
sheen of imaginary words like love, fondness, and faith—
flowery language doesn't leave a good taste in my mouth. I
thought some kind of ray or halo—the kind of halo they
draw around the heads of saints—was pulsing in my loins,
and maybe my sick, tortured halo needed the halo around
her loins and was drawing it toward itself.

"When I felt better, I decided to leave, to lose myself—like
a dog that has contracted leprosy and knows it is going to
die, like birds who hide themselves when death approaches. I
woke up early, put on my clothes, took two cookies from the
shelf, and left without anyone noticing. I ran away from the
misery in which I was submerged. Without any particular
destination, I passed through nondescript streets among the
vulgar, all marked by avarice, chasing money and sex. They

were all just mouths with intestines hanging from them, at the end of which dangled their genitals.

"Suddenly, I felt lighter, more agile—my legs were moving quickly, moving with an unusual nimbleness I could not have imagined—I felt like I had broken all the shackles of my life. I put my shoulders back—this was a natural posture for me. When I was a child, I would do the same thing every time I was relieved from the burden of some chore or responsibility.

"The scorching sun was rising. I went down deserted streets and could see gray houses in strange, geometrical shapes—cubes, prisms, cones—with short, dark, abandoned entrances. They seemed vacant, temporary, as if no living creature could have ever lived in them.

"The sun, like a golden razor, was scraping and removing the shadows off the walls. The alleys extended through aged, faded parapets. All was still and silent. Everything seemed to adhere to the sacred laws of hot, quiet weather. I felt surrounded by hidden secrets, to the extent that my lungs dared not breathe.

"Suddenly, I realized I had left the city gates. The sun's heat sucked the sweat from my body with a thousand mouths—desert shrubs had turned the color of turmeric under the blazing sun. From the depths of the firmament, the fevered eye of the sun cast its burning glance upon the lifeless landscape. But the soil and plants here had a peculiar scent. The scent was so strong it took me back to my childhood—not only did I remember the words and actions from that time but I felt them, as if they had happened just yesterday. I was lightheaded and lucid. The feeling had an intoxicating affect—like aged, sweet wine pulsing through my veins—it penetrated me to my core. I recognized the stones, the trees, the little scrubs of wild thyme, and the thorns of the desert—recognized the familiar scent of the vegetation. I reminisced about those distant days but my memories had wandered sorcerously far and had assumed a life of their own, whereas I remained but a poor, isolated witness. I sensed a deep whirlpool spinning between me and my memories; sensed that my heart was empty and the scrubs had lost the magical scent of those times. The cypress trees seemed to have more distance between them, the hills were dryer—the creature I was before no longer existed. If I prompted him and spoke to him, he would not understand me. He had the face of someone I used to know, but he was not a part of me.

"The world seemed like a sad, empty house, and I felt a tightness in my chest. It was as if I had to walk through this house barefoot and inspect all the rooms. I passed through a maze of rooms but when I got to the last room, *that slut's* room, all the doors behind me slammed shut. Only the quivering shadows of the walls, whose definition had faded, stood on either side, like rows of Black slaves keeping watch over me.

"As I approached the Suran river, a barren mountain appeared in front of me. The dry, hard body of the mountain reminded me of my wet nurse. I don't know how they were related. I passed by the mountain and arrived at a small, pleasant area surrounded by hills. The ground was covered in violet water lilies and on top of the mountain you could see a castle they had built with ponderous bricks.

"I felt tired. I went and sat on the sand at the foot of an old cypress tree by the Suran river. It was a tranquil, pleasing place—I thought, No one has ever set foot in this place before. All at once it came to me. I saw a young girl appear from behind the cypress trees and walk toward the castle.

She was wearing a black dress sewn from very thin, light thread, probably silk. She was chewing the nail on her left hand as she floated by, her movements were effortless and carefree. I thought I had seen her before and knew her—but from this distance and under the glare of the sun, it was hard to be certain—then she suddenly disappeared.

"I was frozen in place and could not move a muscle—but this time I had seen her walk by and disappear with my own eyes. Was she real or an apparition? Was I dreaming or was I awake? I tried hard to remember, but it was in vain. A shudder ran down my spine. It seemed that all the shadows in the castle on the mountain had come to life, and that girl was one of the former residents of the old city of Rey.

"All of a sudden, the scene before me looked familiar. I had come here as a child on the thirteenth day after Now-ruz, my mother-in-law and that slut were here too. We chased each other and played behind these very same cypress trees. Then a group of other kids joined us, but I don't re-member exactly. We were playing hide-and-seek. I was run-ning after this same slut on the banks of this same Suran when she slipped and fell in the river—they fished her out. They took her behind the cypress tree to change her clothes and I followed them. They held a chador in front of her but I was hiding behind the tree and got to steal a peek at her en-tire body. She was smiling and chewing the index finger of her left hand. Then they wrapped her up in a white cloak and spread her black silk dress, which had been sewn from thin thread, under the sun.

"Finally, I lay down on the sand at the foot of the ancient cypress tree. I could hear the sound of the water, it was like the garbled, unintelligible words one hears whispered in a dream. I sank my hands into the warm, moist sand. I squeezed the warm, moist sand in my fists, like the firm flesh of a girl who has fallen into the water and whose clothes have been changed.

"I didn't know how much time had passed. I got up and started walking, but not of my own will. All was calm and quiet. I walked without seeing what was around me—an alien force was prompting me to walk—I was oddly aware of my own steps. I was walking but felt I was gliding along like that black-clad girl. When I came to, I found myself in the city, in front of my father-in-law's house—I don't know why I ended up by his house. His young son, my wife's brother, was sitting on the front stoop—the two were like an apple split in half. He had slanted Turkman eyes, prominent cheekbones, a sensual nose, a narrow, refined face, and had the index finger of his left hand in his mouth as he sat there. Without knowing what I was doing, I approached him, took out the cookies I had in my pocket, and gave them to him and said, 'Your Shah-joon gave these for you.' He called my wife 'Shah-joon' instead of his own mother. He looked at the cookies with his startled Turkman eyes and took them with some hesitation. I sat on the stoop next to him, took him on my lap, and held him close. His body was warm, he had the same calves as my wife, and the same carefree movements. His lips were like his father's lips—but the thing that I found hateful in his father, I found attractive in him—as if his half-open lips had just separated from a long, passionate kiss. I kissed his half-open mouth, which were like my wife's lips— his lips tasted acrid, bitter like the butt end of a cucumber. I bet the lips of that slut had the same taste.

"Then I saw his father—the hunched old man wearing a scarf—come out of the house and walk by without even looking in my direction. He was laughing a halting, terrifying laugh that made the hair of your body stand on end. He laughed so hard his shoulders shook. I was so embarrassed I thought I would melt into the ground. It was close to dusk— I got up as if I wanted to run away from myself. Mechanically, I set off toward home. I could not see anyone or anything—I felt as if I was going through an unfamiliar city. I was surrounded by strange houses in lacerated, geometric shapes with black, abandoned openings—no living creature could have ever lived in them. Their white walls glowed with a ghastly light and the bizarre thing, the thing that I could not believe, was that when I stood in front of them, my shadow, odd and imposing, was cast upon the walls but it had no head—my shadow had no head. I had heard that if anyone sees his own headless shadow, he will die before the year is out.

"I ran into the house terrified and hid in my room. I got a nosebleed and after losing a good amount of blood I passed out on the bed—my wet nurse took care of me.

"Before going to sleep, I looked at my face in the mirror. It was broken, wan, soulless—so wan I could not recognize myself. I went into bed and pulled the covers over my head. I rolled toward the wall, drew in my legs, closed my eyes, and picked up the thread of my reveries—the strands that made up my dark, sad, scary, and enjoyable fate. It was the place where life and death mingled with each other, painting perverted images—old, slaughtered desires, desires that had drowned and disappeared, desires that had been reborn and now screamed for vengeance. At this moment I was severed from nature and the world of appearances and ready to lose myself and be annihilated in the stream of eternity. A few times I whispered to myself: 'Death . . . death . . . where are you?' This soothed me and my eyes closed.

"As soon as I shut my eyes, I found myself in Mohammadieh Square. They had erected a tall gallows and the old oddments guy from outside my window was hanging from it. A few drunken patrolmen were drinking wine at the foot of the gallows. My mother-in-law, with her flushed face, pale lips, and bulging eyes—the same look she would get when she was upset with my wife—was pulling me by the arm through the crowd. She dragged me to the executioner wearing red clothes and said, 'Hang this one too!' I woke up with a start. I was burning like an oven. I was drenched in sweat and my cheeks were on fire. In order to shake off the nightmare, I got up, drank some water, and wet my face and head. I tried to sleep again but couldn't. In the twilight in my room I started to stare at the jug of water on the shelf. I thought that as long as the jug is on the shelf, I will not be able to sleep—I was overcome by a needless fear of the jug falling. I got up to secure the jug, but powerless against my own actions, I intentionally knocked the jug off the shelf and broke it. Finally, I pressed my eyelids together but imagined my wet nurse had gotten up and was looking at me. I clenched my fists under the covers, but nothing unusual had happened. As I was drifting through a coma, I heard the front door of the house. I heard the footsteps of my wet nurse drag her slippers across the floor and go out to pick up some bread and cheese. Then I heard the distant voice of a vendor: 'Blackberries! Cool your gallbladder with blackberries.' No, life had begun in the same tedious way. It was getting brighter. When I opened my eyes, I saw the shimmering image of the sun redirected off the little pool in the yard and reflected on the ceiling through an opening in my room. The previous night's dream seemed distant and distorted, as if I had dreamt it when I was a child. My wet nurse brought in my breakfast. Her face seemed like it was reflected on a hectic mirror, it was drawn and narrow. It seemed comical, as if a heavy weight was pulling down on her features.

"Even though Naneh-joon knew that hookah smoke is bad for me, she kept smoking in my room. In fact, she really wasn't in good humor until she had smoked her hookah. She had told me so much about her house, her daughter-in-law, and her son, that she had made me a partner in all her immodest distractions. Sometimes, for no reason at all—it was so stupid—I would start thinking about my wet nurse's household, but don't know why the lives and delights of others made me retch. In contrast, I knew that my life was coming to an end—slowly, painfully, I was being extinguished. What did the lives of the ignorant and the vulgar have to do with me that I would think about them—they were healthy, they ate well, slept well, and had good sex. They had never felt a speck of my pain, never had the wings of death constantly flap over their heads.

"Naneh-joon treated me like a child. She wanted to examine my whole body. I still felt self-conscious around my wife—whenever she entered my room I would try to cover the phlegm I had coughed up in the pan, I would comb my hair and beard, fold up my nightcap. But around my wet nurse, I was not self-conscious at all—why had this woman, who had no relationship to me at all, gotten herself so involved in my life? I remember in the winters they would set up a korsi[5] by the cistern right here in this room, and my wet nurse, this same slut, and I would all sleep around it. As it was getting light, I would open my eyes and look at the embroidered curtain hanging by the door. The design on it would come to life—it was such a strange and frightening curtain. It showed a hunched old man sitting underneath a cypress tree. He had a turban wrapped around his head like an Indian yogi and held an instrument that looked like a sitar. A beautiful young girl, like Bugam Dasi—a dancer in an Indian temple—with her wrists in chains appeared to be forced to dance in front of him. I imagined that maybe this old man was also thrown into a black pit with a cobra, and that is why he looked the way he did, why the hair on his head and beard had turned white. It was an Indian curtain embroidered with gold thread, and maybe my father or uncle had sent it from a faraway country. Whenever I focused hard on this image, I would get scared. I would wake up my wet nurse who would hold me close to her, with her bad breath and coarse black hair that scraped against my face. That morning when I opened my eyes, she looked the same to me, except the lines on her face seemed deeper and more severe.

"In order to forget, to escape from myself, I often think about my childhood—to experience myself before my illness, to feel healthy. I still felt like I was a child and my death, my annihilation was a second breath that would bring mercy to my state—the state of a child who is destined for death. During frightening moments in my life, it was the calm face of my wet nurse, her pale face, her sunken, unmoving eyes, thin nostrils, and wide, bony forehead that awakened memories of those times in me—maybe she emanated some mysterious ray that soothed me. She had a fleshy mole on her temple with hair growing from it—apparently, I had noticed her mole this day only because I was looking at her so closely.

"Even though Naneh-joon had changed physically, her way of thinking had remained the same. Only, she expressed more of a fondness for life and was afraid of death, like a fly who seeks refuge inside the house at the beginning of fall.

But my life was changing every day, every minute. I felt that for me, the passage of time and the changes people might go through over the course of several years had accelerated by a thousandfold, but any enjoyment I got out of this was inverted and was plunging toward naught and might even sink below naught. There are people whose agony of death starts in their twenties, whereas many others, at the moment of death, gently, slowly, snuff out, like a tallow-burning lamp that has run out of oil.

"At noon, when my wet nurse brought my lunch, I knocked the plate out of her hand and screamed, screamed at the top of my lungs. Everyone in the house gathered outside my room. That slut also came but passed by quickly. I saw that her belly was larger—no, she had not given birth yet. They went and fetched the revered physician—I took great pleasure in having caused trouble for these idiots.

"The revered physician came with his three-span beard and instructed me to smoke opium—what a priceless drug for my painful life! When I smoked opium my thoughts took flight, they became grand, delicate, magical—I was transported to a place beyond the ordinary world. My thoughts were freed from the earthly bonds that weighed them down and would soar toward the calm, dark, heavens. It was as if I were placed on the wings of a golden bat that would fly unencumbered in a radiant, empty world. The effect was profound and satisfying—more satisfying than death.

"When I got up from the brazier, I went to the opening to the yard and saw my wet nurse sitting in the sun and washing herbs. I heard her say to her daughter-in-law: 'We were all on edge, I wish god would just kill him and put him out of his misery'—apparently the revered physician had told them that I'm not getting better. But I was not surprised at all—these people are so stupid! An hour later, when she brought my decoction, her eyes were red and swollen from crying. But in front of me, she would force herself to smile. She would put on an act in front of me—all of them put on an act in front of me—but what amateurs. They thought I didn't know. But why was this woman so fond of me? Why did she consider herself a partner in my sorrow? One day they had paid her to stuff her black, shriveled nipple, like a little penis, into my cheek—I wish gangrene had infected her nipples. Now, when I saw her nipples I wanted to throw up. But back then, I would suck out the essence of her being with a voracious appetite and the heat of our bodies would mingle together. She would fondle me all over and that is why she now treated me with the presumptions of an unmarried woman. She saw me as when I was a child. And who knows, when she used to hold me over the sink, maybe she also pleasured herself on me—the way stepsisters do when they prefer other women for themselves. She would examine me with such curiosity, such precision—'nurture' me, as she would say. If my wife, that slut, had attended to me I would never have allowed Naneh-joon such inroads because I always thought my wife's intelligence and beauty surpassed my wet nurse's. But lust had spawned this sense of shame and modesty in me. In that sense, I felt less self-conscious around my wet nurse—she was the only one who took care of me. Perhaps, she thought it was fate, it was in her stars. Besides, she would take advantage of my illness and confide all her family matters in me. She would narrate their amusements and squabbles, and expose her own unsophisticated, noxious, beggarly soul to me. She was unhappy with her daughter-in-law and talked about her with such hatred, as if she were her rival and had stolen the love and desire of the son toward his mother. Her daughter-in-law must be pretty. I had seen her through the opening to the yard. She had bluish-green eyes, blonde hair, and a small, straight nose.

"Sometimes, my wet nurse would tell me about miracles performed by the prophets. Apparently, this is how she wanted to console me—I envied her degraded, shallow way of thinking. Sometimes she would spy for me. For example, a few days ago she told me that her daughter (meaning that slut) had spent some time sewing a resurrection dress for her baby, for her own baby. Then, it was as if she knew, so she consoled me. Sometimes she goes and fetches me all kinds of drugs and remedies from the neighbors—she will go to the witch, the fortune-teller, the soothsayer. She would crack open the book and consult with them about me. On the last Wednesday of the year, she brought a bowl of augury, which contained rotten onions, rice, and oil. She said she had begged for these as alms with the hope of restoring my health, and she secretly fed me the nasty, disgusting stuff. Once in a while, she also served me the revered physician's decoctions, the same antiaging decoctions he had prescribed for me: hyssop, licorice extract, camphor, maidenhair fern, chamomile, gander oil, linseed, spruce seed, starch, London rocket seeds, and a thousand other kinds of nonsense.

"A few days ago, she brought me a prayer book with an inch of dust on it—it's not just prayer books but any book, any writing by the vulgar is of no use to me. What need did I have for their petty-mindedness and their lies? Was I not the endpoint of a continuous chain from past generations? Did I not have inherited experiences inside me? Did I not carry the past within myself? But things like going to the mosque, the call to prayer, ablutions, prostrations, clearing your throat and spitting, or standing before the mighty omnipotent, the absolute authority with whom one must communicate in Arabic, never had any effect on me. Actually, in the past, when I was still healthy, I had been to mosque a few times—out of obligation. I would try to harmonize my heart with the hearts of others, but the sight of the enameled tiles and the patterns on the walls would carry me off in lucid dreams and inadvertently provide a path of escape for me. When it was time to pray, I would close my eyes and hold my hands in front of my face. In the night that I had created for myself, I would recite the prayers, but the words—like words you repeat unconsciously in a dream—were not coming from the heart. I preferred to talk to friends or acquaintances instead of god—with the mighty omnipotent—because god was too good for me.

"When lying in a warm, damp bed, all these things were worthless to me. At that time, I didn't want to know if a god truly exists or if it is just a personification of earthly power fabricated to solidify the status of some deity and plunder its own subjects. They have reflected an earthly scene upon the heavens—I only wanted to know if I would survive the night or not. Facing death, I saw faith and religion as feeble and childish—almost a kind of entertainment for the healthy and the fortunate—a soul-consuming condition when facing the horrifying reality of death. Everything they had inculcated in me about the day of resurrection and the reward and punishment awaiting the soul was a tasteless deception—the prayers they had taught me were useless before the fear of death.

"No, the fear of death had me by the throat and would not release me—people who have not experienced this pain will not understand these words. The sensation of being alive had amplified in me to such extent that the slightest

momentary pleasure made up for endless hours of palpita-
tion and anxiety.

"I could observe the reality of all the pain and suffering,
but it was devoid of all meaning—I was an unknown species
among the vulgar, to the point where they had forgotten I
used to be part of their world. The horrifying thing was that
I knew I was neither completely alive nor completely dead—I
was a walking corpse who had no relation to the world of
the living, nor could benefit from the oblivion and tranquil-
ity of death.

"In the evening, when I got up from the opium brazier, I
looked out from the opening in my room and saw a black
tree and the door to the butcher shop, which they had
boarded up. Dark shadows mingled with one another—
everything seemed empty and transient. The tarred, black
sky was like a worn chador through which countless bright
stars had poked holes. At that moment, the call to prayer
rang out—a call to prayer at the wrong time. Apparently, a
woman—maybe that slut—was giving birth, was going into
labor. Against the call to prayer, you could hear a dog howl-
ing. I thought to myself: If it's true that everyone has a star
up in the heavens, then my star must be dark, far, and
meaningless—maybe I didn't have a star at all.

"Then the sound of a group of passing, drunken patrolmen rose up from the street. They were making crude jokes
with one another and then started singing with one voice:

> Come on let's go drink some wine,
> Drink some wine from the land of Rey,
> If not now, when shall we drink?

"I pulled away, terrified. Their song lingered in the air; it was haunting. Little by little, their voices grew faint and became silent. No, they didn't want anything with me, they didn't know . . . Once again, silence and darkness besieged everything. I didn't light the tallow-burning lamp in my room. I enjoyed sitting in the darkness—darkness, this viscous element that oozes through everything, everywhere—I was used to it. It was in the darkness that lost thoughts, forgotten fears, and dreadful, unimaginable designs that had been hidden—in I didn't know what recess of my mind—would assume new life. They moved around and taunted me. Everywhere—in the corner of the room, from behind the curtain, by the door— was full of these thoughts and these shapeless, threatening figures.

"There was a frightening figure sitting right there by the curtain. It didn't move; it was neither sad nor happy. Every time I turned toward him, he stared straight into my eyes. His face was familiar, as if I had seen it when I was a child. It was the thirteenth day after Nowruz. I was playing hide-and-seek with the other kids. I think this face had appeared to me along with other ordinary faces—short, pathetic, harmless. The face was like the face of this same butcher across the opening in my room. Apparently, this person has been involved in my life and I had seen him many times— apparently, he was my twin shadow, loitering in the confines of my life . . .

"As soon as I got up to light the tallow-burning lamp, the figure disappeared. I went to the mirror and stared at my face—the image I saw seemed like a stranger—it was preposterous, frightening. My image had become sturdier than me and I had become the reflection on the glass. I thought I could not stay in the same room with my reflection. I was afraid that if I ran away, he would chase me. We were like two cats facing off, ready to fight. I raised my hands and covered my eyes. I wanted to re-create an eternal night in the cavity on the palms of my hands. Fear has often carried a certain intoxicating gratification for me, so much so that I get light-headed, my knees go weak, and I want to throw up. Suddenly, I realized I was standing on my feet—this was very bizarre, it was a miracle—how could I be standing on my feet? I thought if I took one step I would lose my balance and fall over. My head was spinning. The earth and all its creatures were immeasurably far from me. I had a hazy longing for an earthquake or a bolt of lightning so that I could be reborn into a calm, bright world.

"As I was going into bed I kept saying to myself, 'Death . . . death . . .' My lips were sealed but the sound of my own voice frightened me—the courage I had before had disappeared. I had turned into one of the flies that swarm into the room at the beginning of autumn. They cower in the corners, dried out, lifeless, and afraid of the sound of their own buzzing. But as soon as they realize they are alive, they beat themselves mercilessly against the walls until their lifeless bodies fall around the room.

"Whenever I closed my eyes, an obliterated world would materialize before me—a world I had created, a world that conformed to all my thoughts and experiences. In any case, it was more real, more natural than my waking world, and no obstacle could impede my reasoning and my imagination— time and space had lost all meaning. This sense of stifled lust was born of my dreams, born of my secret needs, and the preposterous images and incidents that appeared before me were far-fetched but natural. And right after I would wake up, I still doubted my own existence. I was oblivious of the time and space I occupied—as if I myself was the author of my own dreams and already knew their true interpretations.

"It was late into the night when I fell asleep. Suddenly, I found myself on the streets of an unfamiliar town with strange geometrical houses: prisms, cones, cubes, with short, dark openings and water lilies growing on the walls. I was wandering freely and could breathe comfortably. But the people of this town had died a strange death. They were all frozen in place and two drops of blood had dripped from their mouths onto their shirts. Whoever I touched, the head came off and fell to the ground. I reached a butcher shop and saw a man who resembled the old oddments guy in front of our house. He was wearing a scarf and held a long knife in his hand. He was staring at me with red eyes that looked as if the eyelids had been cut off. I went to take the long knife from him but his head toppled over and rolled to the ground. I panicked and started to run through the streets. Whoever I saw was frozen in place—I was afraid to look behind me. I reached my father-in-law's house and saw my brother-in-law, that slut's little brother, sitting on the stoop. I reached into my pocket and took out two cookies to give him, but as soon as I touched him, his head came off and rolled to the ground. I screamed and woke up.

"It was still twilight. My heart was pounding. The ceiling seemed to weigh down on my head and the walls had turned incredibly thick. My sight had turned dim and my chest was about to explode. I kept staring at the beams on the ceiling, terrified. I kept counting them, again and again. As soon as I shut my eyes, I heard the door. Naneh-joon had come to sweep my room and had put my breakfast in the room upstairs. I went upstairs and sat by the window. From up there

I couldn't see the old oddments guy outside my room, but farther to the left I could see the butcher. His movements, which seemed so fearful, so heavy and calculated from the opening in my room, seemed benign and pitiful from up here—as if he were only acting and was not really a butcher. The emaciated black nags with lamb carcasses hanging from their flanks were coughing a deep, dry cough. The butcher rubbed his greasy hands on his moustache and looked at the lambs with the eyes of a buyer. Then, with great difficulty, he carried two of them and hung them on the hook in his store. He was caressing the lamb's thighs—maybe when he caressed his wife's body at night, he thought of the lambs and imagined how much money he could make if he were to slaughter her.

"When the sweeping was finished, I went back to my room and made a decision—what a horrible decision. I went to the pantry in my room and took the long bone-handled knife out of the box. I cleaned the blade with the hem of my tunic and put it under my pillow. I had made this decision earlier—but hadn't realized it was part of the butcher's performance. When he cut the lamb's thigh into pieces, weighed them, and looked at them with approval, I unwittingly felt I wanted to imitate him—I needed to experience the same delight. From the opening in my room, I could see a deep, blue circle of clear sky through the clouds. I thought I would have to climb a very tall ladder if I were to reach it. The fringes of the sky were covered with dense, yellow clouds that weighed down on the entire town. They were besmeared with death. The weather was dreadful and delightful. I don't know why I was prostrated toward the earth. In such weather, I would always think of death, but now that death, with its bloody face and bony fingers, had me by the throat—now I decided. I decided to take this slut with me so that later people couldn't say of me: 'God bless his soul, he is at peace now.'

"At that moment, they were carrying a coffin past the opening in my room, it was covered in black and a candle was burning at its head. The sound of 'la-Allaha il-Allah,' caught my ear. All the shopkeepers and bystanders were abandoning their own paths in order to follow the coffin for seven steps. Even the butcher took seven steps after the coffin, for the blessing, and then returned to his shop—but the old peddler did not leave his spread. The people had all put on a somber face—maybe they were thinking about the philosophy of death and the afterlife. When my wet nurse brought my decoction, I noticed her knotted brow. She had a string of large prayer beads in hand and with each bead that she counted, she recited her invocations under her breath. Then she started to pray an exaggerated prayer right outside my door, declaiming the Koran at the top of her voice, 'Allahhum, il-Allahhum . . . ,' as if I were the agent of absolution for the living—but none of this buffoonery had any effect on me. Quite the opposite, I loved seeing the vulgar experience what I was going through, even though theirs was fraudulent and temporary, and didn't last for more than a few seconds. Was my room not a coffin? Was my bed not colder and darker than a grave?—a bed that was always made and invited me to sleep. The thought of being in a coffin had occurred to me before—at night I could feel the room shrinking and pressing down on me. Is this how you feel in the grave? Does anyone know how you feel after death? After death, blood stops moving through the body. And after twenty-four hours or so, even though some organs start to decompose, hair and nails still keep growing for some time. Do the senses and the intellect discontinue once the heart stops or do they carry on in some kind of ambiguous life while there is still some blood left in the capillaries? Death itself is frightening enough, imagine knowing that you are dead. There are old people who die with a smile, as if they are going to sleep, or they are tallow-burning lamps that slowly extinguish. But someone young and strong who dies suddenly and his body continues to battle death with all its might—how does he feel?

"I had thought about death and the decomposition of all the particles in my body many times—to the extent that it didn't frighten me—in fact, my true wish was to be completely annihilated. The only thing that frightened me was that the atoms in my body would mix with the atoms in the bodies of the vulgar. This was an insufferable thought. Sometimes I wished that after death I would have long arms and extended fingers with which I could gather all my own atoms and hold them with both hands so that the atoms that belong to me would not enter the bodies of the vulgar.

"Sometimes I thought people who are on the verge of death can also see the things I see. The excitement, the dread, the confusion, the desire to live had ebbed in me. I felt a peculiar calm at having discarded all the opinions that had been drilled into me. The only thing that consoled me was the hope for oblivion after death. I was still not comfortable with life in this world—what use would another life be to me? I felt this world was not for me. It was for a bunch of shameless, offensive, miserly, avaricious muleteers and peddlers of opinion. It was for people suited to this world, people who adulate the powers on earth and the heavens like hungry dogs in front of the butcher shop and wag their tails for a piece of fat. The thought of life only renewed my fear and exhaustion—no, I didn't need to see all these vomitus worlds and miserable faces. Was god such an upstart that he would create his worlds according to my image? But I can't paint a false picture. Even though a new life had to be lived, I prayed for my thoughts and senses to be dull and numb, to breath without effort, without being exhausted, to live my life under the shade of the pillars of a temple of Lingam Puja—I would prowl without the sun hurting my eyes, without the clamor of life and of people's words offending my ears.

"The deeper I withdrew into myself—like a beast that hibernates the winter in some den—the voices of others rang in my ears but I heard my own voice in my throat. The solitude and isolation that hung all around me were as eternal nights, dense and stagnant. They are nights where the adhesive darkness is viscous and contagious, waiting to descend on quiet towns that are full of dreams of lust and hatred. And I— standing on this ledge of my own making—I was the manifestation of absolute madness. The force that glues two people together during procreation in order to ward off loneliness is a result of this same insane disposition that exists in everyone. It is mixed with regret and gently leans toward the pits of death.

"It is only death that doesn't lie!

"The presence of death destroys all superstition. We are the children of death and it is death that rescues us from all of life's deceptions—it is death that calls out to us during life and draws us to itself. At an age when we still don't understand people's language, if we pause in the middle of a game, it is to hear the voice of death . . . throughout life, it is death that is pointing at us. Has it not happened that for no reason you sink into thought and plunge so deep that you become unaware of time and space and don't know what it was you

were thinking about? And then you have to try and familiar-
ize yourself with the superficial world again—this is the
voice of death.

"In this damp bed that reeked of sweat, when my eyelids
got heavy and I wanted to surrender myself to nothingness
and the eternal night, all my lost memories and forgotten
fears would come back to life—afraid that the feathers in my
pillow would turn into daggers; the button on my frock coat
would get as big as a millstone; afraid that the piece of la-
vash bread would fall to the ground and shatter like a shard
of glass; worried that if I fall asleep, the oil from the tallow-
burning lamp would spill on the ground and the entire town
would go up in flames; obsessed that the paws of the dog in
front of the butcher shop would sound like a horse's hoofs;
anxious that the old oddments guy would start laughing in
front of his spread, laugh hard without being able to control
himself; fear that the worm in the footbath would turn into
an Indian serpent; fear that my hands would turn to stone;
fear that my bed would turn into a tombstone and spin on its
hinges and bury me and lock its marble teeth around me;
dread and anxiety that I would lose my voice and as much as
I screamed, no one would hear me . . .

"I always wished I could remember my childhood, but
whenever I did, it felt just as severe and painful.

"There are so many things that are not free of fear and
trepidation: the coughs that sounded like the coughs of the
emaciated nags in front of the butcher shop, having to spit
out phlegm and being fearful of finding traces of blood in
it—blood, this warm, briny fluid, this elixir of life that came
from the depths of the body and would ultimately have to be
expelled—and the constant threat of death that tramples on
any hope of return.

"Life makes each person's masks manifest to himself with cold-blooded indifference. Apparently, each person has several faces. Some constantly wear only one of these masks, which naturally becomes stained and furrowed. This group is frugal. Some reserve their masks only for their own affairs. Others constantly change their faces but as soon as they get old, they realize they are wearing their last mask, which soon becomes frayed and broken, then their true faces emerge from underneath the final mask.

"I don't know what toxin in the walls of my room was poisoning my thoughts—I was sure that before me a blood-drenched lunatic had occupied this room. It wasn't just the walls of my room, but the view of the outside, the butcher, the old oddments guy, my wet nurse, that slut and all the people I would see, the bowl of porridge in which I ate my barley, the clothes on my back—they all had joined force in order to instill these thoughts in me. A few nights ago, as I was undressing in the alcove of the bathhouse, my mindset changed. As the bath clerk poured water over my head, I felt my black thoughts being washed away. In the bath stall, I saw my own shadow on the perspiring wall. I saw that I was just as scrawny and frail as ten years ago, when I was a kid. I totally remembered that is how the shadow of my body would fall on the perspiring wall of the bath stall. I looked at my body closely. There was a hopeless sensuality about my thighs, calves, and genitals—they had the same shadows that they did ten years ago—the same shadows as when I was a kid. I felt that my life, aimless and meaningless, has passed like a vagrant shadow that quivers on the bathhouse wall. But other people were heavy, sturdy, and thick-necked. Perhaps they cast a larger and brighter shadow that lingered longer on the perspiring bath wall—unlike my shadow, which

would disappear right away. When I was putting on my
clothes in the dressing room, my mindset—the way I looked
and moved—changed yet again, as if I had entered a new
world, as if I had been reborn into the same world I loathed.
In any case, I had gained a second life because it was a miracle to me that I had not dissolved like a clump of salt in the
bath stall.

"My life seemed just as unnatural, unclear, and unfathomable as the image on the pen case with which I am writing—
apparently a crazed, obsessive painter had painted the cover
of this pen case. Often, when I look at the image, it seems
familiar. Maybe it is because of this very image . . . maybe
this same image forces me to write. There is a hunched old
man crouching under a cypress tree—he looks like an Indian
yogi. He is wrapped in a cape and has a turban on his head.
He has brought the index finger of his left hand to his mouth
in a gesture of surprise. Across from him, a girl with a long
black dress—maybe she is a Bugam Dasi—holds a water lily
in her hand and dances with mysterious movements. A
stream of water runs between them.

"Sitting by the opium spread, I discharged all my dark
thoughts into that silky, heavenly smoke. At this moment,
my body was doing the thinking, it was dreaming, it was
floating as if I had been released from the weight and filth of
the atmosphere and was flying in a mysterious world full of
mysterious colors and images. Opium had blown a vegetative spirit, a drifting vegetative spirit into my body—I was
traveling in a vegetative world—I had become a plant. But as
I dozed by the brazier on the leather spread with my cloak on
my shoulders—I don't know why—I started to think about

the old oddments guy. He also sat the way I did, hunched
over the stuff laid out in front of him. The thought horrified
me. I got up, tossed the cloak aside, and went in front of the
mirror. My cheeks were on fire and looked the color of the
flesh outside the butcher shop. Even though my beard was
unkempt, I had assumed an attractive, saintly appearance.
My sick eyes looked tired, tortured, and childlike. It was as
if the burden of the earth and of all humanity had been
placed on me. I liked my face. I had discovered this carnal
delight in myself. In front of the mirror I said to myself,
'Your pain runs so deep it is rooted in the depths of your
eyes . . . and if you cry who knows if you will shed any tears
or not.' Then I said, 'You are an idiot! Why don't you do
away with yourself already? What is it you are waiting
for? . . . What do you expect? . . . Isn't there the flask of wine
in the pantry in your room? . . . Drink a cup and be gone . . .
idiot . . . you are an idiot . . . I'm speaking to the air!' The
thoughts that came to my mind had nothing to do with each
other—I could hear my own voice in my throat but didn't
understand the words. The sound of voices mixed with other
voices in my head, like during the times when I had a fever.
My fingers seemed larger than usual, my eyelids were heavy,
my lips had thickened. As I turned, I saw my wet nurse
standing in the doorway. I roared with laughter but her face
did not change. Her gloomy eyes were fixed on me but they
showed no anger or grief. In general, foolish gestures make
me laugh but this laughter was deeper than that—this great
folly was linked to all the other unknown, incomprehensible
things of this world. The thing that gets lost in the dark
depths of the night is the traffic beyond death. My wet nurse
took the brazier and walked out with measured steps. I
wiped the sweat from my brow. There were white spots on

the palms of my hands. I leaned against the wall and rested my head on the pillar—I think I felt better. Then I whispered this song to myself, I don't know where I had heard it before:

> Come on let's go drink some wine,
> Drink some wine from the land of Rey,
> If not now, when shall we drink?

"Right before the onset of a crisis, I always felt a peculiar anxiety that would afflict my gut. It is a mournful anxiety that presses down on my gut—like the weather before a storm. Then the real world drifts away from me and I float in an illumined world, immeasurably distant from the terrestrial earth.

"At this moment I was afraid of myself, afraid of everyone. Apparently, this was related to my illness and that is why my reasoning had become so feeble. When I saw the butcher and the oddments guy from the opening in my room I got scared—I don't know what was so frightening about the way they looked and the way they moved. My wet nurse told me something alarming. She swore to god that she had seen the old oddments guy come to my wife's room at night. From behind the door, she had heard this slut say to him, 'Take off your scarf'—it was inconceivable. The day before yesterday, or the day before that, when I screamed and my wife came to the door, I saw for myself. With my own eyes I saw the old man's teeth marks—his dirty, yellow, rotten teeth marks through which he spewed Arabic verses—on my wife's cheek. Come to think of it, why had this man appeared in front of our house after I got married? Was he sitting in ashes, sitting in ashes for this slut? I remember I went to the old man that same day and asked him the price for his earthen jug. Through the fold of his scarf, two rotten teeth emerged from between his sugary lips—he laughed a dry, disturbing laugh that made the hair of your body stand on end and said, 'You're going to buy without looking at it? This jug is nothing, hah. Take it young man. May it be blessing for you!' Then he added with an odd tone, 'It's nothing, may it be blessing for you.' I reached into my pocket and placed two dirhem and four pashiz coins[6] on the corner of his spread. He laughed again. It was a disturbing laugh that made the hair of your body stand on end. I was so embarrassed I wanted to melt into the ground. I covered my face with my hands and ran back.

"You could smell all the stained and discarded items that had already lived their lives spread out in front of him. Maybe he wanted to show life's discarded things to people, rub it in their faces. Was he not old and discarded himself? The objects on his spread were all dead, they were filthy and broken, but they had such stubborn lives, such meaningful appearances! These dead objects had a profound impact on me, more so than living people ever could.

"But Naneh-joon had brought me the news, she had told everyone . . . with a dirty beggar! My wet nurse told me my wife's bed had lice in it and she had gone to the bathhouse—how did her shadow look on the perspiring wall of the bath stall? I guess it was a seductive shadow with high hopes for itself. But overall, this time I didn't dislike my wife's taste, because the old oddments guy was not the typical daft and dull man who attracts horny women. These pains, these calluses of misery that had crusted on the head and face of the old man and the misery that rained around him—maybe he himself was not aware of this—painted him as a demigod, and the filthy spread in front of him was the manifestation of creation.

"Yes, I had seen the mark of his teeth, his two rotten, yellow teeth through which he spewed Arabic verses, on my wife's cheek—this same wife that would not give me inroads into herself, who humiliated me but whom I loved despite everything, despite the fact that she had never let me kiss her on the lips.

"The plaintive sounds of a kettledrum rose up against the backdrop of a sickly sun. It was the sound of failure that awakens inherited superstitions and fear of the dark. The crisis I was waiting for and the sensation that had previously afflicted my gut finally came. I was burning from head to toe. I was choking. I fell into the bed and closed my eyes—the ferocity of fever made everything seem framed and magnified. The ceiling had moved lower instead of higher. My clothes constricted my body. For no reason, I sat up in bed and whispered to myself, 'More than this is not possible. This is intolerable.' Suddenly, I fell silent. Then, loud and clear, I started mocking myself. 'More than this . . . ,' I said, 'I am an idiot!' I could not understand the meaning of the words I was parroting, I was just enjoying the reverberations of my own voice in the air. Maybe I was speaking with my shadow to soothe my solitude—then I saw something unbelievable. The door opened and that slut walked in. Apparently, she still thought of me sometimes—I am thankful for that. She knew that I am alive, and I suffer, and I will die—I was thankful for that. I only wanted to know if she knew that I was dying because of her. If she did, I would die in peace—I would be the luckiest person on earth. When this slut entered my room, all my bad thoughts flew away. I don't know what ray emanated from her being, from her movements, that so soothed me. She seemed better this time, she was heavier and more mature. She was sporting a gray shirt with embroidered sleeves. She had plucked her eyebrows, was wearing a beauty spot, had put on eyebrow liner, blush, foundation, and eyeliner. In any case, she walked into my room all dolled up. She seemed content with her life and had the index finger of her left hand to her mouth. Was this the same soft woman, the same delicate, ethereal girl with the black pleated dress with whom I had played hide-and-seek by the Suran river—the same girl with the fleeting, childlike air, whose seductive ankles showed from underneath the hem of her skirt? Until now, whenever I looked at her, I hadn't realized. But now, it was as if a veil had been removed from my eyes. I don't know why I started thinking of the sheep in front of the butcher shop—she had become a piece of raw flesh to me and had completely lost her former lure. She had become a ripe, substantial, and colorful woman who cared about life—a complete woman—my wife! To my horror, I realized that my wife had grown up and matured whereas I had remained a child. To be honest with you, her face, her eyes made me feel ashamed. She was the woman who put out to everyone except me—and I could only console myself with imaginary childhood memories of when she had a simple, childish face, and a soft, fleeting quality, and you still could not see the teeth marks of the vagrant old man on her face—no, this was not the same person.

"She mockingly asked me how I'm feeling. 'Are you not free to do whatever you want?' I answered, 'What's it to you how I'm feeling?'

"She slammed the door and left without even turning to look at me—apparently, I had forgotten how to talk to people, living people. I had offended her—her!—the same person who I assumed was devoid of all feelings. A couple of times I was tempted to go and fall at her feet, cry, and ask for forgiveness—yes, cry—because I assumed that if I could cry I would somehow be relieved. How many minutes passed, how many hours, how many centuries, I'm not sure. I had become crazed and enjoyed my suffering—it was a superhuman pleasure, a pleasure only I could feel. Even the gods, if they did exist, could not have had so much pleasure . . . at that moment I discovered my own supremacy. I sensed my superiority over the vulgar, over nature, over the gods—gods born of human lust. I had become a god myself—I was greater than god because I could feel the flow of eternity and infinity in myself . . .

" . . . but she came back—she was not as cold-hearted as I had imagined. I got up and kissed the hem of her skirt and fell at her feet crying and coughing. I rubbed my face on her calves and called her by her real name several times—her real name had a special ring to it. But in my heart, deep in my heart, I kept saying, 'Slut . . . slut . . .' I clasped her legs—the muscles tasted like the butt end of a cucumber, bitter, mild, and acrid. I cried and cried and don't know how much time passed—when I came to myself, I saw she had left. Maybe it didn't even last one second. I felt all the delight, the pain, the caresses of humanity in myself and froze in that state. I stayed there, the same way I sat by the opium spread in front of the tallow-burning lamp—the same way the old oddments guy sits in front of his own spread. I did not move from my place and kept staring at the smoke coming from the tallow-burning lamp—the smolder settled on my hands and face like black snow. When my wet nurse brought me a bowl of barley and rice with chicken, she screamed in horror and backed away and the dinner tray fell from her hands. I was glad that at least I had made her panic. Then I got up, I roofed the wick with the snuffer and went in front of the mirror. I rubbed the smolder all over my face—what a menacing look! I would pull on my lower eyelid with my finger and then let it go, open my mouth wide, inflate my cheeks with air, lift up my beard and curl it from both sides, grimace—my face had the capacity for all kinds of outrageous and intimidating looks. Apparently, this is how I could reveal all the ridiculous, menacing, and unbelievable looks that lay hidden in my nature. I could feel and recognized them in myself, but at the same time they seemed ridiculous. All these different looks were in me and belonged to me— funny faces, scary faces, the face of a murderer—they could all change with the touch of a finger. I could see the face of the old Koran reciter, the face of the butcher, and my wife's face in myself, as if they were reflected inside me—all these faces were inside me but none of them belonged to me. Were the features of my face not caused by some mysterious instigation, by the obsessions, the sexuality, and despondency I had inherited? Was I not the caretaker of this inherited burden? Could I not maintain these looks on my face in a laughable sense of delirium that was out of my control? Perhaps only after death would my face be released from the scruples that bind it and assume it's natural look. But even in that final look, would the ridiculous looks that were constantly abraded from my face, leave their mark, deeper and more severe than before? In any case, I had realized what I was capable of—discovered my talents. All of a sudden, I burst out laughing. It was an abrasive, disturbing, frightening laugh, that made the hair of your body stand on end, because I didn't recognize my own voice. It seemed an alien voice, like the laughter that is often trapped in my throat. I had heard it deep in my ear—it echoed in my ear. Then I started to cough and spat a piece of bloody phlegm, a piece of my liver, on the mirror. I smeared it on the mirror with my fingertip. When I turned, I saw Naneh-joon staring at me. She was pale as moonlight with her disheveled hair and her lightless, terrified eyes. She was holding a bowl of porridge she had brought for me. I covered my face with my hands and went and hid behind the curtain to the pantry.

"I wanted to sleep but felt a tight ring of fire around my head. I could smell the strong, arousing scent of the sandal oil I had put in the tallow-burning lamp. It smelled like the muscles on my wife's legs and I had the subtle, bitter taste of the butt end of a cucumber in my mouth. I was caressing my own body and comparing its different parts—thighs, calves, arms—to my wife's body parts. The lines of her thighs and buttocks, the warmth of her body all manifest before me, but it was a sturdier incarnation because now I needed them. I needed to have her body close to mine. One move, one resolution was enough to drive away this lustful temptation, but the ring of fire around my head got so tight and so scorching it plunged me into a sea of uncertainty awash with terrifying figures.

"It was still dark when I woke to the sound of a group of drunken patrolmen passing through the street. They were exchanging vulgar obscenities and singing together:

> Come on let's go drink some wine,
> Drink some wine from the land of Rey,
> If not now, when shall we drink?

"I remembered. No! It was a sudden revelation that I have a flask of wine in the pantry, the wine mixed with cobra's venom. One cup would annihilate all my nightmares . . . but that slut . . . just the word made me more ravenous for her and made her appear more lively, more torrid before me.

"What could be better than giving a cup of that wine to her, and down a cup myself? Then, after some convulsions, we would die together. What is love? For the vulgar, it is debauchery, it is casual and temporary. The love of the vulgar can be found in foul-mouthed songs, and lewd and licentious expressions that are repeated during drunkenness and sobriety, expressions like, 'sticking the ass's foot in muck,' or 'smearing dirt on the head.' But my love for her was something else. It's true that I knew her from a long time ago—her strange slanted eyes, her small, half-open mouth, her hushed, gentle voice. All these brought back distant, painful memories—in all these I searched for what had been deprived me, what was mine and had been taken away from me.

"Had I been deprived forever? That is why a more harrowing response had been awakened in me, a different kind of gratification to make up for my unrequited love. It had become an obsession—I don't know why I thought of the butcher in front of the opening of my room. He would roll up his sleeves, say 'Bismillah,' and carve up the meat. His gestures were always before my eyes—finally, I made a decision—a horrifying decision. I rolled up my sleeves and took the bone-handled knife from under the pillow. I hunched over and put the yellow cloak over my shoulders, then I wrapped my head and face in a scarf. A mixture of the butcher and the old oddments guy's spirits had manifest in me. Then I tiptoed toward my wife's room—her room was dark—I opened the door slowly. I think she was dreaming—she kept saying, 'Take off your scarf.' I went by her bed and brought my face close to feel her warm, supple breath. It was so pleasantly sultry and rejuvenating! I thought if I could inhale her sultry exhalations for a while, I would come back to life. Alas, for a long time now I had assumed everyone's breath is hot and burning like mine. I looked around to see if there was another man in her room, if any of her fornicators were there or not. But she was alone. I realized everything they said about her was downright calumny and false accusation—who says she still wasn't a virgin? I was ashamed of all my imagined misgivings toward her—I was ashamed of myself. But this feeling only lasted a minute, because at that same moment I heard someone outside the door sneeze and laugh a stifled, mocking laugh that made the hair of your body stand on end. The sound frayed my nerves. If I had not heard the sneeze and laughter, if I had not gotten the omen to wait, I would have cut her up into pieces and given her flesh to the butcher in front of our house to sell to people. I would take a piece of thigh meat as an offering to the old Koran reciter and scream, 'Do you know whose flesh it was that you ate yesterday?' If only he had not laughed—I should have done it that night. That way I wouldn't have to look into the slut's eyes again, because the expression in her eyes humiliated me, it scolded me. Finally, I grabbed a piece of cloth that was next to my foot by her bed, and ran out, terrified. I threw the knife on the roof—because all my murderous thoughts were triggered by this knife—I distanced myself from the knife that was so much like the butcher's knife.

"When I got back to my room, by the light of the tallow-burning lamp I realized I had taken her shirt, the filthy shirt that had covered her flesh. It was a soft silk shirt. It was made in India and it smelled of her body, it smelled of jasmine perfume. The heat of her body, her being, lingered on the shirt. I smelled it, put it between my legs and went to sleep—I had never had such a restful night's sleep. I woke up early in the morning to my wife's hollering. She was yelling about her lost shirt and kept repeating, 'Brand-new shirt!' In fact, the tip of the sleeve was torn, and I would not have given it up even if my life depended on it—did I not have the right to my wife's tattered shirt?

"When Naneh-joon brought me ass's milk with honey and taftoon bread, she had also put a bone-handled knife on my breakfast tray. She said she had seen it on the old oddment guy's spread and bought it. I picked up the knife and looked at it—it was my knife. Then, in a grumbling, offended tone, she said: 'Yes, this morning, my daughter (meaning that slut) says I stole her shirt last night. I don't want to get involved with your problems, but yesterday, your wife saw a stain . . . we knew that the baby . . . she herself said that she got pregnant in the baths. Last night I went to give her a rubdown and saw bruises all over her arm. She said she went into the basement at the wrong time and someone or other pinched her.' She continued, 'Did you know your wife has been pregnant for a long time now?' I laughed and said, 'I guess the baby looks like the old Koran reciter. I guess that's who it takes after.' Then Naneh-joon left the room, all offended. Apparently, she didn't expect that response. I got up immediately, and with trembling hands, put the bone-handled knife in the box in the pantry of my room and shut the lid.

"No, it was impossible that the baby would take after me. It definitely took after the old oddments guy.

"In the afternoon, the door to my room opened and in walked her little brother, this slut's little brother. He was chewing his fingernail. Anyone who saw them would know they were siblings right away. Such resemblance! He had a tight little mouth; fleshy, moist, seductive lips; droopy, half-drunken eyelids; slanted, inquisitive eyes; prominent cheekbones; disheveled hair the color of dates; and a wheat-brown face. He looked just like that slut and had some of her evil spirit. It was the kind of soulless, emotionless, Turkman face that is suited for grappling with life, the kind of face that will do anything to stay alive. Apparently, it was something nature had already predestined, as if their ancestors had lived for a long time under the sun and rain, and had battled nature. Not only had they handed down their looks and character to them with some changes, but they had instilled their own resilience, their own lust, greed, and hunger in them.

"When he came into the room, he looked at me with his inquisitive Turkman eyes and said, 'Shah-joon says that the doctor said you're going to die. And we'll get rid of you. How do people die?'

"I said, 'Tell her I've been dead for a long time.'

"'Shah-joon said that if I had not lost the baby, the whole house would have been ours.'

"I started laughing uncontrollably. It was a dry, disturbing laugh that made the hair of your body stand on end. I didn't recognize my own voice. The child ran out of the room, terrified.

"At that moment I understood why the butcher got such pleasure out of wiping the bone-handled knife on the lamb's thigh. It was the pleasure of cutting the flesh in which dead, coagulated blood had pooled like slime and dripped from the lamb's throat onto the ground. The yellow dog in front of the butcher shop, the severed head of the cow lying on the ground that looked out with unfocused, bulging eyes, and also all the lambs with the mist of death covering their eyes, they all had seen this and they all knew.

"Now I understand that I had become a demigod. I had stepped beyond people's petty, immaterial needs. I could feel the stream of eternity flowing through me—what is eternity? For me, eternity meant sitting by the banks of the Suran and

playing hide-and-seek with that slut, and for just one moment, closing my eyes and hiding my head in her lap.

"Suddenly, I realized I was talking to myself, but in an
odd way. I wanted to talk to myself but my lips were so
heavy, they couldn't make the slightest movement. I felt I
was talking to myself without moving my lips or hearing my
own voice.

"In this room that was like a grave and got darker and
more cramped by the second, night surrounded me with its
gruesome shadows. I sat in front of the smoldering tallow-
burning lamp wrapped in a fur-lined coat, a cloak and a
scarf—and my shadow rested on the wall. My shadow on
the wall was more vibrant, more defined, more real than my
true self. Apparently, the old oddments guy, the butcher,
Naneh-joon, and my slut wife had all been my shadows at
some point, shadows among whom I was imprisoned. At
that moment, I looked like an owl but my cries were knotted
in my throat and I spat them out like bloody phlegm. Maybe
the owl also had an ailment that made him think like me.
My shadow on the wall looked just like an owl, bent over
and reading all my writings closely. He probably knew
well—only he could understand. When I looked at my shadow
from the corner of my eye, it frightened me.

"In this dark, still night, like the night that had engulfed
my entire life, fearsome figures made faces at me from every
corner, from behind the curtain. At times, my room would
get so small that I felt I was lying in a coffin. My temples
were on fire, my limbs could not endure the slightest movement. There was a weight pressing down on my chest, like
the weight of the carcasses being delivered to the butcher,
draped over the necks of emaciated black nags.

"Death was gently whispering its song, like a mute who

has to repeat every word and as soon as he gets to the end of a single verse, has to start from the beginning again. Its song penetrated the flesh like the vibrations of a screeching saw. It screamed out and suddenly went silent.

"I hadn't closed my eyes yet when a troop of drunken patrolmen passed by my room. They were exchanging vulgar obscenities and singing together:

> Come on let's go drink some wine,
> Drink some wine from the land of Rey,
> If not now, when shall we drink?

"I said to myself, in any case, I will finally fall into the hands of the sheriff!—suddenly I felt a superhuman strength inside me. My forehead cooled down. I got up and threw my yellow cloak over my shoulders and wrapped my scarf around my head two or three times. I hunched over, went and took the bone-handled knife I had hidden in the box, and tiptoed toward the slut's room. When I got to the door, I saw the room drenched in dense darkness. I listened carefully and heard her voice:

"'Are you here? Take off your scarf.' Her voice had a pleasing ring to it. It was like her voice when she was a child, like untroubled whisperings in sleep. I had heard this voice before in deep sleep—was I dreaming? Her voice was muffled and hoarse, like the voice of the little girl who played hide-and-seek with me by the banks of the Suran. I hesitated, and again heard her say:

'Come in. Take off your scarf.'

"Slowly, I entered the darkness of the room, took off my cloak and scarf, and got naked—but don't know why—I got into her bed with the bone-handled knife still in my hand. It was as if the warmth of her bed had given me new life. Then I embraced her warm, dewy, delightful body and remembered the pale, skinny little girl with the large, innocent Turkman eyes with whom I had played hide-and-seek by the banks of the Suran. No!—I attacked her like a wild, ravenous animal. I hated her from the bottom of my heart—love and hatred had become intertwined. Her cool, moonlit body—my wife's body—opened up and trapped me inside her, like a cobra coiled around its prey. The scent of the perfume on her breast was intoxicating. Her arm that was wrapped around my neck had a delicate warmth. In this moment, I wished my life would end because all the spite and hatred I felt toward her had disappeared—I was trying hard not to cry. I didn't even notice but she locked her legs behind mine and grasped the back of my neck with her hands like a mandrake. I could feel the alluring heat of her juicy flesh, I drank up this heat with every atom in my body. I felt her draw me into her as if I were her prey—I was overcome by a mixture of dread and delight. Her mouth tasted like the butt end of a cucumber; it was bitter and acrid. I was under the command of all the atoms in my body. They were singing a song of victory at the top of their lungs. And I, feeble and condemned, was tossed in the waves of an endless sea of lust and longing, and bowed my head in submission. Her hair, which smelled of jasmine perfume, was glued to my face—a chant of joy and fear rang out from the depths of our beings. Suddenly, I felt her bite down hard on my lip, so hard that she split it in half—is this how she chewed her finger as well, or did she realize I'm not the old man with the sugary lips? I wanted to flee but it was impossible to even budge—all my effort was in vain—the flesh of our bodies had been fused together. I thought I had gone mad. In the midst of the struggle, I inadvertently moved my hand and felt the knife I was still holding sink somewhere into her body—a warm liquid splattered on my face—she screamed and released me. I clenched the warm substance that had pooled inside my fist. I threw away the knife and rubbed my free hand on her body—it was completely cold—she was dead. In the middle of all this I started to cough, but it wasn't a cough—it was the sound of a dry, disturbing laugh that made the hair of your body stand on end. Terrified, I threw my cloak on my shoulders and returned to my room. In front of the tallow-burning lamp, I opened my fist, I saw her eyeball in my hand and my entire body was covered in blood. I went to the mirror but was so afraid I had to cover my face with my hands. I saw that I resembled—no, I had become the old oddments guy. The hair on my head and beard was like the hair of someone who had just been brought out of a room with a cobra—it had all turned white. My lip was split like the lip of the old man, my eyes had no lashes, a clump of white hair showed on my chest, and a new soul had entered my body. I thought and felt in a completely different way and could not escape from him—escape the demon that had been awakened in me. With my hands in front of my face I burst into uncontrollable laughter, it was stronger than before and shook my entire being. It was a profound laughter and I had no idea from what hidden pit in my body it was coming from. It was a hollow laugh trapped in my throat that poured out of some abyss—I had become the old oddments guy."

The force of my anxiety made it feel like I had just woken from a long, unfathomable sleep. I rubbed my eyes, I was in the same room as before. It was twilight and mist covered the windows—you could hear a rooster crowing in the distance. In the brazier in front of me, the glowing charcoal had turned into cold ash and could be blown away with one breath, and my thoughts were as empty and ash-light as the spent charcoal that could be blown away with one breath.

The first thing I looked for was the flower vase from Rhages that I got from the old wagoner in the graveyard, but it was not there. I looked by the door and saw someone with a bent shadow, no, it was a hunched old man with a scarf wrapped around his head and face. Under his arm, he had something that looked like an earthen jug wrapped in a filthy piece of cloth—he laughed a dry, disturbing laugh that made the hair of your body stand on end. As I went to move, he left my room. I got up and wanted to run after him and take the earthen jug wrapped in cloth from him—but the old man moved away with unusual nimbleness. I went back and opened the window to the street—I saw the old man's hunched figure in the street. He was laughing so hard, his shoulders shook. He had the bundle under his arm and moved away, falling and rising, until he completely disappeared in the fog. I went back and looked at myself. My clothes were torn and I was covered from head to toe in coagulated blood. Two golden bee flies were flying around me and little white maggots wriggled on my body—and the weight of a dead body pressed down on my chest.

Notes

1. Nowruz is the Persian new year and is celebrated on the vernal equinox. The thirteenth day after Nowruz is referred to as "Sizdah bedar," and marks the end of the new year celebrations. On this day, families typically picnic outdoors.
2. *Shabdolazim* is a shrine and cemetery in the city of Rey. It is named after Abdol Azim al-Hassani, also known as Shah Abdol Azim, who was buried there in the ninth century.
3. *Qiran* and *abasi* are coins that were in circulation in Iran until the early 1930s.
4. The term translated here as "cobra" is from *Naja*, the scientific name for a genus of venomous elapid snakes known as cobras. It is derived from the Sanskrit word *naga*, a semidivine, half-human, half-snake figure in Buddhism, Hinduism, and Jainism.
5. A *korsi* is a low table with a thick blanket draped over it and a heating element, traditionally a brazier with hot coals, under it. Before the advent of modern heating in homes, families would keep warm at night by sleeping around the *korsi*, with their legs under the blanket that covered the *korsi*.
6. *Pashiz* and *dirhem* are coins that were in circulation during the Sassanian Empire (third century CE).